RULES OF DUEL

RULES OF DUEL

Graham Masterton
with
William S Burroughs

First published in the UK in 2010 by
Telos Publishing Ltd
5A Church Road, Shortlands, Bromley BR2 0HP,
UK

www.telos.co.uk

Telos Publishing Ltd values feedback. Please e-mail us
with any comments you may have about this book to:
feedback@telos.co.uk

Cover Art: Lee Thompson
Editor: Sam Stone

This Edition 2014

ISBN: 978-1-84583-856-0

British Library Cataloguing in Publication Data.
A catalogue record for this book is available from the
British Library.

Introduction

William Burroughs was living in Tangier in 1964 when I first wrote to him. I was 18, a trainee newspaper reporter in Crawley New Town, in Sussex, England.

I had been asked to leave school a year before – not for any serious breach of school rules but because I was supposed to be studying English literature, which meant the English heritage of Shakespeare and Milton and Alexander Pope. Instead, I had become enthused by the 'Beat' writing of Jack Kerouac and Allen Ginsberg and Gregory Corso and Lawrence Ferlinghetti, among others.

When I was supposed to be reading *Love's Labour's Lost* and *Lycidas* and *The Rape of the Lock*, I was engrossed in *On The Road* and *Howl* and *Gasoline* and *Pictures of the Gone World*. I wasn't in Illyria with Orsino. I was crossing the Mid-West with Dean Moriarty.

I loved and respected Shakespeare and Company. But to me, as a young man in the early 1960s, the Beat writers were living and breathing and they seemed to see the world in the same way that I did. They were anarchic, they were angry, they were political. Sometimes (by the standards of the time) they were obscene. But at the same time they were lyrical and sentimental and they saw the beauty and significance in ordinary people and everyday life.

I didn't look like your typical Beat, although I did habitually wear tinted spectacles. I was a Mod, which meant that I was always snappily dressed in tailor-made suits with narrow lapels and button-down Oxford shirts with neckties as skinny as snakes. And chisel-toed Italian shoes. Dressing like that was revolutionary then. In Carnaby Street, apart from John Stephen's new menswear store on the corner, there was only a traditional tobacconist and a greasy spoon café.

The notoriety of *The Naked Lunch* preceded its first publication in Britain in 1964 by John Calder. I managed to buy a copy almost as soon as it was published (42 shillings) and I was deeply impressed. William had shown that, without realizing it, we were all living on a nightmarish planet in which bureaucracy was trying to suffocate everything funny, everything irreverent, everything spiritual and everyone who wouldn't or couldn't conform.

Of course it was also a novel about drugs and homosexuality, with some wildly scatological humour. But you didn't have to be a gay junkie to appreciate the serious (and not-so-serious) thinking behind it.

The Naked Lunch and the novels which followed it were a bitter attack on intellectual censorship and the restriction of individual freedom. Like the new satirical TV shows which sprang up in the 1960s, they attacked the establishment by mocking it and yet also by showing how oppressive it was.

William wrote back to me almost immediately, and over the next year or so we regularly exchanged postcards and letters. I was already writing poetry and novels and I was extremely interested in what he called 'intersection writing'. This was an extension of a technique which he had developed with the artist and novelist Brion Gysin, in which he had cut up columns from newspapers and magazines and rearranged them to make new sentences.

Intersection writing was less mechanical than cut-ups and depended on the writer to look for ways in which to interchange words and phrases to bring out new meanings. You would look for coincidences in names and places. You would look for a way to take half of one sentence and attach it to another, to give a totally different or a more descriptive view of the same event. It was shaking up words like the particles in a kaleidoscope, and constantly creating new patterns.

William moved to London in 1966 and rented a top-floor apartment in Duke Street St James's. By that time I had finished my newspaper training and found a job as deputy editor of a new British men's magazine, *Mayfair*, a blatant imitation of *Playboy* and *Penthouse*. 'Deputy editor' sounds a much grander position than it actually was. The staff comprised the publisher, the editor, me, a secretary and the publisher's Labrador.

Now that William was living in London I was able to meet him face-to-face for the first time, and we met regularly for dinner or just to talk. He was droll, he was polite (except when he had drunk a little too much Scotch), and he was endlessly interested in all kinds of social and political control. He believed that big business had conspired to suppress any invention that threatened their profits. He said that an everlasting light bulb had been patented, but the patent had been bought up by large American electrical corporations, and locked away forever. He claimed that one small company had invented everlasting socks, which he had worn for years in South America, but the clothing industry had made sure that they were discontinued. He believed that General Motors had made sure that the revolutionary Tucker Car never went into mass-production.

At that time, William was fascinated by Scientology, and it occurred to me that he should write an investigative article about it for *Mayfair*. He and I travelled down to the Scientology headquarters in Sussex and entered the building under assumed names – William Lee and Graham Thomas.

That was the beginning of long series of articles which he wrote for me – *The Burroughs Academy*. Each month he wrote a think-piece on social disorder or new ways of controlling the human mind or how to improve your intellect. Some of the articles were reprinted in Daniel Odier's book of interviews with William, *The Job*, and you can still find the entire series on the internet. Eventually they formed the basis for his book *The Wild Boys*.

At the same time, I was keen to write my own intersection-style novel which depicted London as it then was. I had already discussed with William an idea which had been given to me by the late Piero Heliczer, the avant-garde film-maker – *Rules of Duel*, which was the title of one of Piero's poems. The concept of *Rules of Duel* was to describe the terms of engagement between the establishment and the free-thinkers – what we used to call the 'counter-culture'.

Rules of Duel started its life as a scattering of chaotic notes and poems, but William was always enthusiastic about the idea and even included several sentences from *Rules of Duel* in his novel *Nova Express*. When he came to London I was able to develop the idea into a novel. We would sit in his apartment over a meal that was served by a sulky young boy with L-O-V-E tattooed on his knuckles, and talk over the novel's setting, the characters, and whole concept of intellectual guerrilla warfare. William decided that he was going to be Motherwell the Everlasting Executioner. Many other characters in the book are based or partly-based on real people of the time.

On some evenings, other Beat writers would turn up. I talked about *Rules of Duel* with Allen Ginsberg and Alex Trocchi and Brion Gysin, too. Brion said it was time for London to be given 'the treatment'.

William wrote an introduction for *Rules of Duel* which was also an explanation of intersection writing. This year I came across his original typescript, which had been stored away in my library for forty-five years. I thought how long ago those evenings in Duke Street now seemed to be – yet how oppressive and illiberal the world still is – and how we have allowed our bureaucracies to control our thinking and micro-manage every detail of our lives.

So maybe it's time for *Rules of Duel* to see the light of day again, and maybe it's time for us to renew the challenge for our personal freedom and our intellectual independence. As William wrote in *Nova Express*: 'Who monopolized Immortality? Who monopolized Love, Sex and Dream? Who monopolized Cosmic Consciousness? Who monopolized Life, Time and Fortune? Who took from you what is yours? Listen all you boards syndicates and governments of the earth. Pay it all back. Pay it all, pay it all, pay it *all* back.'

Graham Masterton,
January 2010

Foreword
William S Burroughs

1. IN THIS FOREWORD for *Rules of Duel* I have endeavoured to clarify an 'entertainment' I call 'intersection reading' right where you are sitting now Mills Bros ash tray on the table about the colour of the map of Tangier which is on or more precisely under the glass cover on this table which is ideal for work being five feet square. You come to where I finished carrying a Lettera 22. New connection Franklin (as in typewriter) (Underwood) (second hand). Now just *here* by my left hand (end joint of little finger missing is a file labelled *The Captain's Log Book*. February 5, 1899. On the cover is a burning ship the *Lakonia* if my memory serves. On the cover part of a torn page. I read: 'In life used address I give you.' Top floor of the lottery building, Tangier, 16 Rue Delacroix. Across the street is the Tanger Hotel (They have taken the *i* (*I – red* remember, from Rimbaud's *Colour of Vowels*) they have sucked the *i* out of Tanger sad dead empty. Across the street is the Tanger Hotel which used to be the Pasadena Hotel and the bus still has *Pasadena* Hotel written on it. And just *here* by my right hand is an aerial photo of Tangier before they

cut down all the trees in the Large Market. At the end of the table on my right is a copy of *Minutes to Go* and just *here* under the aerial photo SEPTEMBER AFTERNOON *'I wait in pieces smoking over the summer pavement.'* So sitting here in my brocade armchair. I pick up a Penguin edition *In Hazard* by Richard Hughes who also wrote *A High Wind In Jamaica.* I open the book to Sunday page 139. I read: *'Just at that moment Sparks appeared on the bridge to report his emergency set was once more working.'* Turn to page 140 and I read: *'"Send a call to all ships" said Captain Edwardes,'* (yes I knew an Edwardes when I first came to Tangier years ago. He died of an OD (overdose of junk) in Madrid) *'"Estimate position so-and-so, require immediate assistance." And keep on sending.'* Sparks with blanched face departed on his ominous duty. Now this intersects one of my characters from work in progress tentatively entitled *A Distant Hand* Lifted I quote from memory: 'Sweating fear like a vice just telling you Sparks is over New York.' Now just here is a picture from *Newsweek* May 18, 1964. A plane I mean in pieces. A priest there hand lifted *Last rites for 44 airliner dead including pilot Clark (left) – and their murderer.* In 1957 or thereabouts I wrote: 'An old junky selling Christmas seals on North *Clark* Street … "The Priest" they called him.' *Transatlantic Review* 15 page 58. Now the Priest hustled his score money stealing suitcases … *EXPECTANCY on intersection valise* … Intersection reading and writing an 'entertainment' from *Graham* Greene to *Graham* Masterton Gossop's *Green* connection Bill Franklin Monument 21380 187 West 101 Street New York from Pitman's Common Sense Arithmetic Monument 15 New York to *'Abdulla 16!'* A sort of book code do you see *messages travelling along intersections?*

2. LAST AUTUMN...OVER THE LAST SKYSCRAPERS A SILENT KITE

September 17, 1899

over New York

This foreword to
Rules of Duel by Graham
Masterton is an essay in
'intersection reading '
right where you are sit-
ting standing walking
now. When you read look
listen think precise in-
tersection points right
where you are reading
now look round..tip-tap-
ing of a dripping faucet
Do you have a dripping
fawcet? I do in this
room on the top floor of
the lottery building
Tangier. Needs a new
washer. Speak to the por-
ter. He sits on a bench
downstairs. We step qui-
etly into the street a
man plays Pasadena on an
old record player PASA -
DENA. You got it? When
I step quietly into the
street so as not to stir
the ambulant vendors and
guides, there is a bus
of the PASADENA hotel...
(Boat whistling in the
harbour) past the green
dentist remember the old
dentist from Graham
Greene's The Power And
The Glory? Still there
waiting last boat whist-
ling in the last harbour
here and there the glow
of drift wood fires sun-
lit chimneys of North-
road Brighton Shift to
The Moving Times My Mag.
published by J. Nuttall
37 Salisbury Road Barnet
Herts London 'as I know
from my blind wait betw-
een London and Brighton

full moon... violet even-
ing sky... over the empty
broken streets a red whi-
te and blue kite..piece
of a toy revolver there
in nettles of the alley

Now the Moving Times was
a preliminary experiment
in what I called inter-
section reading right
where you are sitting
standing walking now just
here is a letter from
Graham T. Masterton'I was
in Notting Hill Gate when
I read it corner of Lad-
broke and Goldborne Roads
contacted Bill Franklin.
As in type writer..second
hand..Underwood..Monument
15..New York..flickering
tele from Abdulla 16..
Sour visions, Mr. Bradly
Mr. Martin decaying hands
on your desk sausage roll
coffee Remember the pri-
vate detective from Gra-
ham Greenes Ministry of
Fear? sausage rolls cold
coffee right where you
are sitting now your sad
captains Mr Bradly Mr Mar
tin dim jerky far away
traced this format from
Time May 15, 1964 page 38
if my memory serves pic-
ture of kite duel between
male and female kites..
fighting kites cost up to
18$.. Superman last aut-
umn over the last skyscra
pers a silent kite I can
see the picture quite
clear from my balcony..

a sundown newsstand flap
ing against the cool gl-
ass of autumn windows...
the old pond under the
leaves intersection val-
ise waiting for contact
in the broken streets
Dim jerky far away stars
splash his cheek bones
with silver ash. In life
used address I give you.
Cool remote Sunday...its
a long way to go..see on
back each time place what
I mean dim jerky far away
...not present except in
you reading the intersec-
tion points right where
you are reading now. So
look listen remember as
you read.. nettles under
the railway bridge rain
washed condoms..dead wasp
in rancid sunlight..Heinz
57 baked beans tomato
sauce stains his Player
rust colored wine (Yes
Ian Sommerville just
poured it)

List of Characters

<u>Staff of 'The Evening Waistcoat'</u>
Tom Crisp, reporter
Reporter A14
Rufus Shack, reporter
George Macfries, night editor
Ron Holland, industrial reporter
Arthur the Laugher Smith, double agent.

<u>Staff of Tin Type Hall</u>
Hilary Starfessed, executive manager
Paul Szondi, psychiatrist
Motherwell the Everlasting Executioner
John Remorse, the Serjeant of Time Film
Gordon Casper, photographic assistant
Mozart, Berlioz and Wagner, secret agents.

<u>Other characters</u>
Samuel Baptist, HM Inspector of Brothels
Charlie Bowdre, owner of Victorian Naughties
Monsieur Retaud, professional assassin's victim
Janine Blown, one of Retaud's mistresses
Gaylord Smith, ditto
Dr Cary, world expert on halitosis
Johnson Willow, music vendor
William Turner, former abortionist turned actor
Mrs Binfield, brothel madam
Workman Bill, workman
The Famous Ear, workman
The Captain of Kodak, photographer
Jack Beauregard, the Eater of Cities

LIST OF CHARACTERS

Dolores Beauregard, his mother
Killick-Cullip, his schoolmaster
Cecil Brolac, baby-shop manager
The Silver Vicar
Bridget Segrave, alias The Girl
Marsha van Doepnts, Szondi's former wife
Dolores Shallott, a six-foot-nine Jewess
Peter Hostess, manager of Big Bang Remedy Ltd
Enox, head of the Ugly Family
Margaret, his wife
Eric Goodbody, liaison man for the Ugly Family
Alfred Waltz, bank clerk
Black Rod
Detective Inspector Gallagher
Charles McFee, his assistant.

<u>And also featuring</u>
Doctor Who, Nubar Gulbenkian, Walt Disney, Margaret
Drabble, The Duke of Edinburgh, Marcello Mastroianni,
Batman, Captain Marvel, Mandrake the Magician, the
Green Hornet, Rafael Nightingale the Sinister Armourer
of Curzon Street, Immodesty Blaze, J Paul Getty,
Aristotle Onassis, Dick Tracey, Flash Gordon, Teddy
and the Pirates, J D Salinger, Mr Lim Kim Guan of 'The
Straits Times', Prince Albert, Tiffany Jones, Jimi
Hendrix, Shirley Temple, Hughie Green, Marlene
Dietrich, Isadora Duncan, Lord Baden-Powell and
many others.

The action takes place over four days in South London.

1

yes, we have no bananas

Jack Beauregard the Eater of Cities is a marked man and he knows it.

The wires tell him the Famous Ear tells him. All around, on posters and signboards, the words come that Jack Beauregard is a marked man. Everybody knows and they stay clear of him. He doesn't talk to anybody any more – just paces the streets of London with the whites of his eyes roaming and his hands in his raincoat pockets.

And you can see him anywhere, a suburb in his pocket and a city on his leg, picking his teeth with a factory chimney. He sits in the dingy Formica coffee bars of Brixton and Streatham with his hard eyes hidden by his hair, sipping carefully a cup of cold tea. He is a tall, stooped man, and they're after him. His eyes are sunk into his bony, indeterminable face. He is wearing his old demob suit, and is permanently high on cardboard.

(You can smell him, Jack Beauregard. He smells of

dust and burning cardboard, with a dying hint of mothballs.)

They're after him and they'll have him by 4:00pm. Everybody knows and already he's as good as finished.

Charlie Bowdre rings me up and says: 'They're after Beauregard. He's wearing his old exploding pavements and the smell of wires. Dying hint of suburbs – his eyes are sunk into mothballs.'

'I know,' I tell him, swivelling round in my newspaper office chair. 'I phoned Tin Type Hall this morning, but there was no reply.'

No reply no reply for Jack Beauregard. He's on the corner of Cromwell Road and Cornwall Gardens. He's moving East. He stops to look at a weighing machine. The trees pass the traffic passes.

He drops a penny into the weighing machine and it tells him in a cold, electrode voice: 'You weigh 11 stone 13 pounds and they'll get you by 4.00pm.'

He moves on. He doesn't bother to look round any longer. He's so transparent you can see the red of the passing buses through his raincoat. He lights another factory chimney and puffs nervous industrial fumes into the fading day.

He's been around longer than anyone can remember, Jack Beauregard. His name first became known in connection with the Lethal Postmen Scandal in 1938 – and since then he has somehow been tied with every major disaster in the world. There are still persistent rumours that he was entirely responsible for the Second World War.

He denies these saying: 'It was an accident. A few people are bound to get hurt in every accident.'

But even for a man like Jack time runs out. There are few natural deaths for the envoys of Tin Type Hall.

He doesn't bother to look round any longer. You weigh the city and there are still persistent postmen. He moves on into nervous industrial accident. 'A few people are bound to see the red of passing electrode.'

Ron Holland, our industrial reporter, is following Beauregard closely. He phones in progress reports every few minutes from call boxes all over London. I take them where I sit in my smoky office overlooking the Holborn Viaduct.

'He's moving towards Knightsbridge now. The streets are almost empty. He's staying out in the open but that won't stop them. He's trying to keep within sight of policemen as he goes.'

Elimination on tracks for Jack Beauregard. The sky is dark for this time of day. Strange electric buzzing shifts through the office. Down in the concrete basement the muffled beating of the presses, printing the Late Extra of The Evening Standard.

'Ron, is that you?'

'*Où se trouve* Dick Tracey? *Où se trouve* Flash Gordon?'

Mothball elimination for this time of day. He's moving into Green Park. He's moving into Piccadilly Circus. He's keeping out in the open. Strange electric policemen phone in smoky basements. Is that you? Remember the late extra Tin Type Hall.

It's 3:58pm. There are two minutes to go. Ron doesn't phone any more but stays a few yards away from Beauregard as he walks into Haymarket. The day is grainy and photographic. There's the scent of rain in the air. Jack in his tired old overcoat keeps walking among the crowds. Could almost feel Cold Sun. The noise of traffic is blurred in strange electric film. He paces the eyeballs with elimination on tracks. There are two minutes to go.

The phone rings and I scoop it up. It's Rufus Shack, ringing from a callbox in Leicester Square. He says hurriedly: 'A large car – suspect it belongs to Tin Type Hall – moving toward Haymarket. Keep on alert.'

The phone rings again. It's another reporter, from Venables Street, outside entrance Tin Type Hall. 'Could almost feel Cold Sun. The day is strange electric park. Suspect it belongs to demob death.'

One minute to go. Ron Holland closes behind as Jack Beauregard the Eater of Cities closes towards flashpoint. Shoulders hunched, his raincoat flapping in the sooty London draught. The question of work was four to six months before. 'I have seen butchers at work in shops showing as much emotion as he did when they were cutting up sheep's ribs.'

Thirty seconds. Three large cars move into Haymarket on all sides. 'He was very calm indeed. He was not in a frenzy … no frenzy at all.' The light is failing and you can hardly see the faces of the drivers as the cold cars approach.

'This is it,' over distant electrode intercoms. The sweep second hand reads 4:00pm. 'Did he give any indication as to how?' Panic elimination in the dark. Jack Beauregard instinctively dives for cover.

You must remember how he spoke. That was days before, a cool February afternoon with the sky the colour of pale glue. He was driving his car through Kensington – his eyes shifting from traffic to road and across to Gerald Musgrave, who was sitting beside him with his hands clasped in his lap.

'The art of good driving,' he was saying, 'is to have a louder horn than anyone else.'

The horn in his car had been specifically designed

for him by Flugelhorn of Mayfair. It was a tape recording of a bull moose in heat, mingled with jet noises from London Airport and the amplified farts of a thousand fruit flies.

This was his special car. At the flick of a switch, it could be turned into a street side Oyster Stall complete with two lifelike plaster customers. From the twin exhausts, it could fire a mixture of limestone and molasses, guaranteed to incapacitate all pursuers. The seats were fitted with high-speed electric drills, so that in a desperate situation the driver could tunnel his way under the road, and catch the nearest Underground to freedom. Beautifully finished in anodised blue, the car was capable of 150mph, and could be driven underwater.

'It cost a bomb,' says the old doctor, driving it carefully into Charlotte Street and parking outside his cut-rate dentist.

This was his special farts. It was a tape recording of Jack Beauregard in heat, mingled with underwater oysters. The amplified drills of a desperate situation. From the twin flies, a mixture of pale glue and cut-rate customers. You must remember how he could tunnel his way to freedom.

'Did he give any indication as to how?'

'Is that you?'

Beautifully finished Jack Beauregard, the Eater of Cities. The day passes the traffic passes. Guaranteed a 1000mph.

So we wait in cold office for further news of the Mysterious Babies. There is nothing running. The few reporters left in the newsroom sit reading and smoking with cups of tea on their desks. The noise of the presses has subsided, and there is only the sound of a single typewriter clattering away down the corridor.

There is no plot. There is no news. Our front page lead today is the story of an elderly widow who killed her Pakistani lodger with a poisoned steam pudding.

'He kept eyeing me all the time,' she said. 'Did he give any indication as to how …?'

I am anxious when the lines are quiet. The day is brooding slowly into a wet, miserable evening. The sodium street lights flicker pink, and gradually the rood of the city fade. It is so quiet you can hear the cleaners breathing as they polish the empty news desks. You can hear their disinterested hands over the copy like the feet of deer among leaves. Occasionally one of them coughs, or a match flares. You never see them. They come in like ghosts, clean the building and go. I sometimes think there are no cleaners.

It is 7:30pm or 8:15pm. The clock on the wall has tricked me. I walk over and switch on the lights and the building is like an old cavern. It is so quiet you can hear their disinterested ghosts like the feet of evening with a poisoned widow.

'*Où se trouve* Dick Tracey? *Où se trouve* Flash Gordon?'

I ring in Tin Type Hall again but the lines are blocked. There is strange electrode interference on the wire. I put the phone down and wait for the passing sky.

FLASHBACK TO HAYMARKET: Where the cars are moving in on silent wheels. Jack Beauregard the Eater of Cities dives slow motion for cover. It's an old dive, the dive of a practised gunman. The body twists to the right and the knees buckle gently. The left shoulder swings, shifting him to shop doorway cover. But it's too slow – the dying years weighing on his move.

'Is that you?' It's Charlie Bowdre on the phone again. He's an old contact of mine, famous for his Original Victorian Follies. He has a moustache like a 1910 aviator.

'Yes – Crisp here. What've you got for me, Charlie?'

'It is the concept if the girl's plentiful bosom shows, old boy. Only become an evening of guilt. Affair with a girl before you'd a place where actual physical costumes will be seen. Just telling you.'

'Have you seen Cold Sun?'

Charlie Bowdre dwindles on GPO lines. It was his 60th birthday last week. He ordered an exploding cake from Rafael Nightingale, the Sinister Armourer of Curzon Street.

'You'll be delightfully surprised,' said Raphael with a slow smile. 'When I make exploding cake, I make EXPLODING cake.'

Charlie grunted and said: 'Leave off the marzipan. Marzipan I hate. And it's so difficult to get off the chandeliers after the bang.'

The idea of the cake was to blast the clothes from all the women in the room. Charlie's plan was to blow a whistle so that all the men could dive for cover behind the sofa, then push down the plunger and start an orgy. Unfortunately the cake blew the sofa with 11 distinguished guests clinging to it, into a nearby public convenience.

'It was a bet,' Charlie explained to the police. 'We are seeing how many distinguished people we could blow into the loo at one go.'

I keep trying all my contacts all over London, but the wires are empty. The city is peopled with phantoms. Just telling you I'm worried about the movements of Tin Type Hall. It shifts from street to street like a moving sand dune. The Mysterious Babies are back and we know it. Fear is perched with the starlings on the telegraph wires of the city. Dark electric buzzing fills the sky.

'Have you seen Cold Sun?'

'Just telling you he kept eyeing me all the time.'

FLASHBACK TO HAYMARKET: And Jack Beauregard is nearly at the shop door. A look of bewilderment and agony slides over his face. His eyes roll slowly from side to side. His hand instinctively moves to his shoulder holster, but for years he has kept nothing in there but cigars. He fires Havana into the blurring street.

Outside Tin Type Hall our reporter keeps a constant watch with directional microphones and long-range camera devices. He senses that something is wrong and gives me a call at the office. I sip my late-night coffee and listen to his urgent voice.

'Two cars just left here. They disappeared down Venables Street and into the Bayswater Road. Both had dark windows so I could see nothing. I suggest you alert Ron Holland and Rufus Shack.'

'Suggest nothing. Everything is under control. Just concentrate on the picture and the story. I want you back in here by 11:30pm.'

I grow nervous and tense. I walk about the office picking up paperclips and putting them down again. I stare out of the window but there is nothing to be seen across the street except the dim light of the coffee bar. I light a cigarette and slump back in my chair.

Mysterious Babies trying to take over the city. Directives from Tin Type Hall warble like doves in the fading sky. The four-second pulse of the nuclear warning signal touches our nerves. Just ready for whatever might occur.

Mysterious Babies you must remember crowding in the mind's rim. Last seen disappearing through the frosted glass door. Their plan somehow connected with Tin Type Hall, which is the most powerful organisation in the city. It controls everything from gas, water and electricity to free school meals and refuse collection.

'We even have a dustmen's choir,' a Tin Type Hall representative is alleged to have said.

Unfortunately the cake blew the electric death. Blow a whistle so that the frosted gas could disappear in his slow movement to the door. They clean the office and go. You must remember the mind's representative.

Tin Type Hall shifts from street to street, changing address and telephone numbers with each move. It is impossible to pin down. Before any major deal, there is unusual activity in this way. We suspect that the Mysterious Babies are back in the city.

'Actual physical costumes will be seen. What've you got for me, Charlie? The push the plunger to start a takeover.'

Just as I am giving up all hope, Ron Holland rings to say that Motherwell the Everlasting Executioner has been seen in St James's Park.

State opening of the Houses of Parliament. It is being televised for the first time, so the crowded benches of the Commons are full of fresh haircuts and shiny shoes. There is a rustle of expectancy in the musty House, and outside you can hear the burble of the crowds of sightseers.

The House is brightly lit, and uncomfortably hot. The glass eyes of the television cameras are screened behind velvet curtains. The MPs glance at them nervously and adjust their ties.

The Speaker looks bored under his ratty wig. From time to time he peers nearsightedly down the central aisle to the main doors. He looks at his watch and it reads 4:00pm.

'It was right by the BBC this morning,' he says worriedly to Labour front benchers.

Sitting with his legs crossed and three inches of white leg exposed, the Prime Minister chats in an undertone to the Chancellor of the Exchequer. The Chancellor nods enthusiastically, and nudges the Home Secretary, who is sweating quietly into his pinstripe waistcoat.

The Opposition benches are almost empty. The few MPs scattered sparsely on the old cracked leather seats are wearing Mickey Mouse masks and feathers in their hair. The Shadow Cabinet have dressed in gold lamé suits with two-tone shoes and purple handkerchiefs in their breast pockets.

'Don't take any notice of them, Jim,' the Prime Minister whispers to the Chancellor. 'They're only trying to attract attention.'

'Could almost feel Cold Sun.'

After a few minutes, the muttering begins to die, and the members look expectantly towards the doors. There is the sound of footsteps from outside, and a murmur of 'Action' from the TV men above.

Black Rod, dressed in full regalia, comes walking slowly to the doors of the House. In his hand, instead of his rod, is a brand new electric cleaner. He carries it with dignity and poise, and ignores the sudden buzz of alarm from the Commons benches.

The official at the door turns white. He tries to

slam the door in Black Rod's face, but Black Rod shoots his foot into the gap and stops him. He peers around the crack with his pale, indeterminate face, his eyes darting blankly over the House.

'Can I interest you in a vacuum cleaner?' he says blandly.

The official, trembling, opens the door for him. He walks quietly and calmly to the centre of the House, while the MPs watch him in amazement.

Black Rod surveys the members coolly. Then he says: 'I see you have quite a cleaning problem here. Have you ever felt that your old machine wasn't doing the place justice?

'If so, just take a look at this. This cleaner is the very latest model at 65 guineas. It has 145 different attachments, including devices to inflate your car tyres, cook four-course meals, construct a cantilever bridge in 11 minutes, destroy pet spaniels with ease and efficiency and suck registered letters out of post boxes.

'Gentlemen, buy your wife this cleaner for her birthday and she won't forget you. Now I'll just show you exactly how much dirt your old cleaner left on these floors by running over them with this.'

Black Rod plugs in the vacuum cleaner and moves round the House, nozzling away the dust. When he's finished he empties the bag on to the table next to the Mace and smiles triumphantly.

'Right then,' he says, 'down to business. The Queen commands your presence in the House of Peers, so biff off and listen to what she's got to say.'

Interviewed afterwards by a reporter from the Daily Mangle, Black Rod comments: 'I can't afford to live on my Parliamentary stipend alone. I also sell copies of Old Moore's Almanac if you'd like to buy one.'

But we suspect this is a further move by Tin Type Hall to penetrate into power. We put a tail on Black Rod and watch for his contacts.

Motherwell the Everlasting Executioner rides into the city like Jesus on a bicycle. Old newspapers blow under his wheels like palms.

He is humming his favourite tune as he rides, 'Jeannie with the Light Brown Hair.' His face is cold and strange, and his long dusty coat flows behind him. His hands on the bicycle are blue, and glow softly in the dim light of evening. His legs hardly seem to move, yet his old bicycle wheels speedily along Westminster Embankment, the chill of the river blowing across to deserted Parliament Square.

He parks the bicycle under the trees, and takes off his clips. He looks at his watch. Then he melts slowly into the clotting dusk until you can hardly see him. Only a faint disturbance in the air and the sound of his footsteps betray his presence.

'She's my Jeannie with the light brown hair,' he hums.

He carries in his pocket, as you may know, the Programme of Sliced Man. It is drawn out in filaments of bank-note metal on watermarked paper, and he has it safely in a waterproof oilskin pouch. It vibrates softly the new plan of the Mysterious Babies.

Motherwell shifts swiftly to Trafalgar Square by process of old movies. He avoids the traps and humming detectors. He avoids the electricity of the city.

'How much does it cost to fall through an open manhole?'

'Only a cover charge. Drop in sometime.'

The Programme of Sliced Man is one of the most

sinister of Tin Type Hall's new devices. It is based on the action of film, as all their actions are based. This is all we know. Maximum security at Tin Type Hall has fallen like a gray mist. The towers of the building are seen only dimly through the stagnant trees.

It is drawn out in filaments of clotting dusk. His legs hardly seem to sound, yet the traps of light brown hair move with him over the open charge. 'Drop in sometime'.

The man who told us about it is Alfred Waltz, a bank clerk at Putney. He was working at his till when Tin Type Hall representatives came in for an unspecified amount of bank-notes.

It is late as Alfred locks up his drawer with jangling keys and prepares to leave the bank. The sun is setting the trees on fire, and a band of orange light falls across the floor.

He looks over to the manager's office. Behind the frosted glass Mr Blomfeld still has his desk lamp alight. Alfred walks over and taps on the door.

'I'll be going now, sir,' he says shyly.

The manager's blurred image looks up. 'Righto, Waltz. Before you push off, put these in the vaults for me.'

Mr Blomfeld opens the door. He is a fat man, with a pinstripe waistcoat drawn tight across his stomach. In the waistcoat pocket, a fat watch ticks. He hands Alfred a stack of files and smiles briefly.

'Very good sir,' says Alfred, as the door closes.

Waltz clatters through the empty bank, breathing quickly. He goes out by a side door and down a short flight of steps to the vaults. He takes out his keys and unlocks the vast steel door in the wall.

The vault door is specially designed to relock

itself automatically if the person who enters is wearing scent. It is the pride and joy of Mr Blomfeld, who sends young secretaries down there on fictitious errands. Once they are trapped in there, he takes his monogrammed contraceptives and a bottle of Sanatogen tonic wine and spends the afternoon.

The door only failed once, when Blomfeld re-opened it, wine and condoms in hand and his tongue hanging out, to find his managing director there.

'I – er – thought you might like a drink, sir,' said Blomfeld hastily. 'And these were all I could – er – find to drink it out of.'

'I was frightened to death, dear,' said the managing director as he stormed out. 'It was like being stuck in a ghastly great ladies' loo.'

Alfred has to use both hands to prise open the door. He picks up his sheaf of files and steps into the green gloom of' the vault. His footsteps echo. On all sides, on rack after rack, are neatly tied bundles of bank-notes. The smell of them is like ether. They reflect green on Alfred's face.

Alfred unlocks the inner barred gate and continues into the depths of the strong room. He is just putting away the files when he hears a sudden crash behind him.

FLASHBACK TO HAYMARKET: As Jack Beauregard the Eater of Cities crumbles across the pavement with bricks and windows showering slow-motion around him. He raises a torpid cloud of dust that clings in the air like the stain of ink across paper. His hands grope for the concrete of old cities.

Alfred unlocks the inner barred image and clatters into the empty waistcoat. He hands Alfred a ghastly contraceptive. The pocket of it smells like ether.

The green gloom failed only once, when fictitious secretaries wearing his pride and joy.

'Welcome to my humble abode.'

'Now you come to mention it, it is pretty frowsy. Come to think of it, you're not looking too good yourself.'

Alfred steps the green bank-note. Remember the bricks and windows based on the action of film. It is drawn out in filaments of bank dust. He carries in his pocket as you may know a river of ink. He is just putting away the files when it is pretty frowsy. Welcome to my humble security.

'Hard-boiled eggs and nuts! Mmmm-mmmm!'

Alfred's vision becomes suddenly restricted. He is unable to see anything except for a small blurred circle in front of his eyes. He tries to raise his head but there is a silent vibration that pulls his muscles slowly downwards. He feels he is moving underwater. Every gesture takes agonising minutes to perform.

Through the fading hallways of bank-notes floats Motherwell the Everlasting Executioner, his big black Luger in his hand. His eyes are swallowed in impenetrable darkness.

'Drop in sometime.'

'Remember I could feel Cold Sun.'

Alfred sinks to the floor, hardly able to breathe. He sinks into the dry sea of money. He gropes about on the concrete like a dying diver. Motherwell hovers over him with a bitter smile. His whole body is a bitter smile.

'What's the matter, Alfred?' he says in his distant, reedy voice.

Alfred can say nothing. He is being absorbed in the clinical nostrils of old anaesthetic. He is now lying with his cheek against the floor, and a web of spittle joining his mouth to the files. His eyes are rolled back into his head, exposing the whites. They tremble like underdone eggs.

'You let me down, Alfred,' continues Motherwell. 'You didn't do as I asked. I'm afraid you're on the list now, sweetie.'

He eases the catch of his Luger and points the cold muzzle against Alfred's ear. It is chilly in the vault, no sun ever reaches it. It is fed only by the frosty breath of perishing bank robbers.

Motherwell becomes aware of a rustling around him. It is like a phantom hand riffling down the bank-notes. He looks up quickly, his eyes swivelling about the vault, but it is deserted. The rustling is like the feet of deer among leaves.

The noise grows louder. It blows from end to end of the strong room, with increasing frenzy. And yet there is no wind, and the dust of a million bank-notes poises still in the air.

Motherwell stands up, jerks nervously from one wall to the other, his gun wavering and his eyes dark. He claws at a handful of bank-notes and they shimmer green in his hand. It's the green that's after him. Green film threat blowing cold and deadly through the old vault.

'He kept eyeing me ...'

He fires wildly into the stacks of money. The ear-splitting blast of his Luger makes the room jump. Shreds of green paper fill the air. He reloads with quivering fingers and walks from top to bottom of the vault, blazing his gun into the bundles of bank-notes.

When the noise subsides, the strong room looks like the scene of a pillow-fight. Motherwell moves through the smoke and floating paper to Alfred.

The body is gone. There is only a heap of rapidly-decaying cheques and invoices. An unseen wind blows them across the floor and between the bars of the iron grille.

We are walking quickly through Kensington Gardens. We feel a thunderstorm is coming on. The grass is a bright, wet green through the deserted trees. The sky overhead is a vivid khaki.

We crunch briskly along the centre of the wide, gravelled path. In front of us, and behind us, a line of strangers in various raincoats also walk down the centre of the path. They are equally spaced fifty yards apart.

The first fat droplets of rain. Across the smoky sky, with an electric tearing noise, a jet airliner approaches London Airport from the West. I notice a building, surrounded by little bushes, that appears to be half-built. A geometric pattern of white scaffolding, and the zinc smell of thunderstorm in the air.

We walk on down to Exhibition Road. The people are still in front and behind. Last year at Marienbad. Albert in his old Memorial stares at Entrance 6 of his sooty red Hall and can never go in, not even for the Bob Dylan concert.

(There was hot sunshine in January, and sea, and a man was saying indistinctly: 'I'm glad I don't like spinach, because if I did I'd eat tons of it, and I can't stand the stuff.' He advances and recedes in waves, like a transistor radio on the beach.)

Remember the mind's representative. Remember to turn left at the corner, carrying with you your old photograph of rugby captains. Mysterious Babies move in with new Sliced Man Programme, code name Beauregard.

Gordon Caspar, captain of the Knightsbridge Archipelago, has a job with the old sage of Kodak. He works eight hours a day removing the genital triangle from nude photographs with a chinagraph pencil.

'I reckon I get through about 200 vaginas a day,' says Gordon, pausing for a moment in his chemical-smelling darkroom to talk to our reporter.

He lives in a large Victorian hostel near East Grinstead, and drives into town every day in his battered Ford Zephyr. He reminds me vaguely of Buster Keaton – same expressionless face and hard white cheekbones.

Our reporters search his dark-room closely for any sign of the Sliced Man Programme. They take 15 negatives and pay Gordon £10 for them. They are locked up in the office safe of the Evening Overcoat for future reference.

Evening falls along the westbound roads of London. We walk down Kensington Gore, past the plane trees, keeping an eye open for red telephone boxes. The traffic is thinning, and the green streetlights are flickering on.

'Is that you?'

'Only become an evening of guilt.'

The hostel where Gordon Caspar lives is in misty, spacious surroundings near the Weir Wood reservoir. It is a large grey stone building, dated 1874, and the gardens have fallen into neglect. Outside the kitchens, in the long grass, the bird-picked bones of beef. Strange decaying smell of English countryside.

He comes to the door when we ring. We follow him into the dark hallway, overlooked by crumbling balconies. He leads us upstairs, to the top floor, where the ceiling has skylights, cluttered black with leaves.

The rooms have been repainted like a seaside boarding house mostly a pale sea green. There is bright wallpaper and contemporary divans in the enormous, half-empty rooms.

On the attic wall I find a bell panel, with names still visible under the grime. It reads: Lord Keith's Dressing Room; Lady Frewen's Drawing Room; Nursery for Lord Martin. I have a small twinge of regret for England. Gordon is calling us from his bed-sit room.

FLASHBACK TO HAYMARKET: As Jack Beauregard slides claws drifts to the pavement, and his loose change rolls silently across the road to spin and pirouette under the feet of passers-by and the wheels of the cars of Tin Type Hall. His mouth begins to draw open to shout or to say something, but it is so slow and long that I can no longer make out what he is saying –

Pressure has been mounting over the cities and the Pay-TV network. A spokesman said: 'Gas discoveries, daughter. I'm not saying the housewife would butcher the grocer.'

It is a gray evening in a Sussex chalk quarry near Hayward's Heath. The cold wind riffles through the weeds and Queen-of-the-May, and a few spare gulls shriek over the grimy white buttresses of limestone.

On a box, near a small privy, sit Workman Bill and the Famous Ear. They are hefty, and rough, and dressed in thick overalls. Their coarse voices are sucked away by the wind. Workman Bill is fumbling with a liquorice cigarette paper and Old Holborn that keeps flying away. The Famous Ear is drinking reflectively from a thermos flask.

'Bugger,' says the Famous Ear.

Workman Bill is just licking his tatty cigarette,

and as he opens his mouth to answer, the wind blows it down his throat. He washes it down with tea, and starts patiently to roll another.

'Bugger,' says the Famous Ear again.

'What's up with you, then?' asks Workman Bill.

'Nothing. I was just thinking.'

'Well, what you say that for?'

'What did I say what for?'

'What you just said.'

'I didn't say nothing. I was just thinking, wasn't I?'

'Oh,' says Workman Bill, and carries on with his cigarette. His greasy curls are already flecked with shreds of tobacco, and the ground around him is strewn with cigarette papers.

'Very nice bit of sandwich, this,' comments the Famous Ear.

'What you got in it, then?'

The Famous Ear lifts open his half-eaten sandwich to have a look. He sniffs at it and closes it again. 'Bloody fish-paste, I think. I keep telling 'er not to give me bloody fish-paste.'

Workman Bill says: 'Don't you like fish-paste then?'

'I wouldn't ask her not to give it to me if I liked it, would I?'

'No, 'spose not.'

They sit together in the quarry as the breezy sun sinks lower, filling the crags of chalk with violet shadow. Their eyes cast ruminatively about. Workman Bill begins to smoke and the smoke floats through the grass.

Finally, the two men stand up, brush down their overalls, and stretch. Then they walk over to the privy and unlock the rusty padlock on the door. Plastered on the inside of the hut are dozens or nude photographs from 'PARADE'. There is no lavatory, but a tangled heap of nitranite explosive belts, almost 140lbs of it.

'What are we going to blow up tonight, then?' says Workman Bill, looking thoughtfully at the bright orange sticks.

'That old bint what lives over the dry cleaners in West Road,' says the Famous Ear. He takes a grubby pencilled map out of his pocket, and points to it. 'We'll need about 25lbs, mate. Put it in your sack and follow me up to the car.'

They drive off towards the town as the streetlights are coming on. They say very little. Occasionally, Workman Bill takes out his petrol lighter and relights his dwindling cigarette. The Famous Ear keeps his eye on the road.

They park their Commer van outside Revivers Dry Cleaners and get out. The Famous Ear walks over to the door in his chalky boots as Workman Bill lugs out the explosives.

'Are you there, mother?' bawls The Famous Ear, hammering on the glass shop door. 'Are you up there, you old bat?'

They wait side by side in the fading street. Eventually, a light comes on inside the shop, and the door is unlocked. The woman stands there in a flowered overall, enormously fat, with her piggy eyes glittering at them.

'What do you want?' she says abrasively.

The Famous Ear is inside the shop immediately. He takes the canvas satchel from Workman Bill and holds it up. 'In here, mother, we've got the finest cut-rate corset you've ever seen. Just imported, under the counter, of course, but I thought you'd like to have first refusal.'

'You've got your refusal,' grates the woman. 'No.'

The Famous Ear rubs his chin and leans against a rack of dry-cleaned trousers.

'Mother,' he says, 'don't throw away the chance of a lifetime. These will bring back your vanished youth. You'll get a real bang out of them.'

With a dramatic flourish, he takes out the belt of nitranite and holds it up.

'Funny colour, ain't they?' she says.

'Madam, madam,' says the Famous Ear, 'these are the latest exciting colours from Paris. Just imagine your husband's face, jaded after years of seeing the same old pink scaffolding, when he claps his peepers on these. Fiery tangerine, this colour's called. Want to try them on?'

'All right, you've convinced me,' growls the woman. She hitches up her skirt over her gigantic white thighs and steps into the belt. Workman Bill is giggling like a maniac, and The Famous Ear pushes him out of the shop, where he continues to laugh until he nearly chokes.

The woman strains herself slowly into the belt. There is sweat on the Famous Ear's face as she drags them over her rump. Then finally she has it on, and breathes a vast, hot sigh of relief.

'They're not very comfortable,' she says, patting her stomach.

'They will be, mother, when they're in action, so to speak,' says the Famous Ear. He takes up the trailing fuse in his thumb and forefinger, and lights it with Workman Bill's lighter.

'I suppose I'll get used to them. Just let me go and

look in a mirror,' adds the woman, and shuffles off into the gloomy back of the shop, trailing the sparkling fuse.

FLASHBACK TO HAYMARKET: As Jack Beauregard the Eater of Cities gropes for the kerb, a thousand years of buildings falling from his shoulders. His scream is like the dull, thick sound of a hammer falling in a water tank. His undersea eyes fall gradually across the darkening sky.

Motherwell, as you know, is carrying his Sliced Man Programme through Kensington Gardens. His smile freezes the trees. His whole body is a cold smile. 'Just telling you to drop in sometime.'

The love affair. It's so dark in the bedroom that you can see only their eyes. The amplified sound of their hands moving over the sheets, and the wet click of parting lips. Occasionally their whispers break the silence.

'VA NOSVESENSKY DASCHA, FJEWO IN GASCA.'

'BLOMNIV RE PETASCH.'

Flickering subtitles read: 'I am worried about – what he is going to say when he finds the tractor.'

'He keeps eyeing me.'

(It was so hot I could scarcely look at the sea. There was a boat out there somewhere, but it was dissolved in a sheath of light. I lit a cigarette and sat on a rock. Someone whistled.)

They painstakingly reconstructed the crime. Detective Inspector Gallagher and his wan assistant, Charles McFee, carefully putting together the bits of dry cleaners' shop and fat woman. They used a meat chart they borrowed from a nearby butcher's.

'I have seen a butcher display more emotion when cutting up a sheath of love. Occasionally they drop in sometime.'

'Is it you?'

It is a gray evening in his wan assistant. Workman Bill is just lighting the overalls. They park their piggy eyes in the dwindling glass of 'PARADE'. There is no nude photograph, only the Famous Explosive with his eye on the road.

'The suspects are in the house next door.'

'There is no house next door.'

'Then we'll build one.'

What he is going to say when he finds the tractor. What is he going to say when the old bat takes a grubby pencilled sack from 25lbs of bright orange youth. 'You've got your refusal.' Just remember the map's assistant.

Mysterious Babies their new plan. The wind of August is blowing the flies from the door. Say nothing. The traps are closed. There is a strange electric buzzing in the air and it is impossible to tell if the sun will rise again.

Inter-galactic conference at Tin Type Hall. The zinc smell of Alfred in the air. They are putting their plan into operation and we are unable to get through. I dial Tin Type Hall every half hour throughout the evening and there is no reply.

(The signs of the explosion are removed silently and swiftly by the Big Bang Remedy Co., an organisation that has its headquarters close to Venables Street, headquarters of Tin Type Hall.

Big Bang is owned by Peter Hostess, who made his money selling theatrical rifles to Israeli forces during the Sinai crisis. When they were fired, a flag popped out of the barrel, reading: 'SORRY! THE REAL RIFLES HAVE GONE TO HARROW DRAMA

SOCIETY! JUST THINK HOW THEY FEEL!'

The company has a fleet of green removal vans, which arrive on the scene of the explosion like a flock of hawks as soon as the smoke has cleared. They rapidly construct a cardboard facsimile of the original building, and disappear. They are green and silent. They do their work and go.

'By now,' says Peter Hostess, wearing a turquoise jacket and sucking a pink cigar, 'over half of England is a cardboard facsimile.')

Detective Inspector Gallagher arrives on the scene of the crime on a rusty tandem. He motions his assistant to hold it while he looks round the building. He sees no sign of damage, only hears the Cold Sun crackling behind the clouds.

'Just telling you it was all a mistake.'

'Could almost feel Cold Explosion. Drop in sometime.'

The detective leaves, creaking off into the marmalade sunset on his old machine, his assistant panting red-faced behind him. 'I killed my grandmother this morning,' he says, just for the sake of saying something.

'Oh, I'm sure she had it coming to her, sir,' says the assistant politely. The smile of Motherwell leers out from a hedgerow.

Again, the love affair. The first cracks of morning light glinting through the curtains. The girl sighs and turns over, still asleep. I look at her through the sticky corner of my eye, and touch her shoulder.

(The sea was warm when I stepped into it. A Chinese fishing boat dipped out slowly into the Straits of Johore. Out in the twinkling water, the incessant noise of insects was left behind ...)

Again, the love affair. It is impossible to tell any longer where we are. It is so silent. The Captain of Kodak is peering round the door, taking photographs with his Instamatic camera.

(Remember that I am still a prisoner in the concrete cells of Tin Type Hall. I have been here for over a year now, and there seems to be no possibility of release. My food arrives when I am asleep, and I have seen no-one for over three months.)

Monsieur Retaud, the professional assassin's victim, has suddenly materialised from Bulgaria, where he was hired to be shot by an extremist faction who were demanding that advertisements for foundation garments should be removed from the city's Metro.

(The girl, with her thin, dark-eyed face, puts her thumbs in her tiny white panties and steps out of them. The manager of the hotel surfaces from the bathwater in full evening dress and says: 'Is there anything else you require, madam?')

Retaud decides to hold his annual banquet a little earlier this year. He invites over 900 people, including Nubar Gulbenkian, J Paul Getty, Aristotle Onassis, Walt Disney, Margaret Drabble and the Duke of Edinburgh.

The banquet is held in Retaud's country house, just outside Horsham. The gardens are decorated with coloured lights, and the French windows are opened so that the music from the orchestra drifts out across the chilly evening lawns.

(The girl's pale nipples begin to revolve. The manager stands knee-deep in hot water and fires at them with a large pistol. A chambermaid rushes in, and is shot in the side of the head and lies on the tiles bleeding.)

The guests assemble in the glittering banqueting

hall. Mirrors on every side reflect the lines' of magnificent tables, beautifully laid out with silver cutlery and condiments, and decorated with fresh-cut roses.

Monsieur Retaud walks in, followed by his faithful mongrel Shipshape. The hound follows him as if on a string. Retaud orders it to sit, and faces the enormous company, already buzzing with conversation.

He raps the table, and silence falls. Heads are lowered. Monsieur Retaud mumbles: 'Grace, please.'

He says: 'Dear God, for what we are about to receive, may you make us truly thankful. And may the company assembled here today not worry that the chef who cooked all the food is a leper.'

There is thunder of chairs, and the guests sit down. Monsieur Retaud is on the upper table, flanked on one side by his latest girl-friend, Janine Brown a pallid woman with eyes like poached eggs, and a Baron with a tubercular cough and a wild gray moustache.

The staff silently moves round the hall, serving the melon à porto. The guests have been fasting all day for this meal, since Retaud's banquets are famed for their sumptuousness, and the rumbling of empty stomachs makes the salt cellars rattle.

It is only after a few minutes that realisation dawns on the guests that Retaud is playing one of his elaborate practical jokes. The melons, instead of steeped in port, are filled with Esso motor oil.

Retaud smiles vividly to everybody around, but nobody stops eating. It is obvious that only Retaud's favoured guests are eating genuine food – and nobody wants it known that they are only clingers-on in his social circle.

'A very nice 20/40, if I may make quite so bold,' whispers the Baron with a cough. Monsieur Retaud nods, and gives another flashing smile.

Slowly, concealing their disgust behind their napkins, the guests finish the melon. The waiters whip the plates away and serve the soup.

The soup doesn't taste so bad. The guests gulp it down with plenty of bread, and some of them even begin to cheer up. They even manage to ignore an old ex-Mayor, who lit a cigarette to take the taste of the melon away, and now has dense black clouds of oil smoke issuing from his nose and mouth.

'No, no, I'm quite all right,' explains the Mayor hastily. 'It's just a little internal trouble I picked up in the First War. I swallowed a smoke bomb. It recurs from time to time. Heh, heh, serves me right for facing the Bosch with my mouth open.'

'A splendid soup,' the Baron Whispers to Monsieur Retaud. 'I am unfamiliar with it, though.'

Monsieur Retaud grins again. 'Just a little something the chef thought up. It was either that or having the cats put away.'

The banquet continues, growing in size and atrocity. The waiters bring on course after course of fried rats, poison toadstools, chicken giblets, bones, fat, gristle and garbage. Many guests have fallen from their chairs and are lying, green-faced, on the floor. Several of them are violently sick on to the table, and it becomes hard to tell which is food and which is vomit.

Retaud himself sits pulling his fine black moustache and sucking on a pheasant bone. He pinches the breasts of his girl-friend Janine and giggles to himself. On the other side, the old Baron has fallen with his face in a great helping of earthworms and OK sauce.

Finally, still munching on a pear, Retaud climbs up on to the table and walks down it, stepping carefully to avoid the dishes and cutlery, painting his guests with a large brush and a pot of green emulsion paint.

At the end of the lower table, he turns round and walks back again, jumping on his guests' hands and fingers. Eventually he grows tired and drops back into his seat.

He slings his arm round his mistress, and she begins to squirm out of her clothes, until she is dressed in tight black corsets and suspenders and nothing else.

But as he kisses her, a chill draught blows under the door.

Windows begin to bang open and shut all over the house, and the lights flicker dull and green. It is as if a frosty hurricane had entered the building.

Motherwell, the Everlasting Executioner, removes his latex mask of the Duke of Edinburgh and rises slowly from his place at the table. His appearance raises nothing but groans from most of the guests, who have passed out all over the banqueting hall in various postures.

'Monsieur, monsieur,' whispers Motherwell in his high-pitched effeminate voice. It is a voice that tastes of train whistles and railway timetables. 'That's the shittiest meal I've tasted since Johnny Robbins got caught up in a corned-beef mincer. Sweetie, you'll have to do better than that.'

Retaud has turned white. He pushes his girlfriend away from him and crouches, trembling, behind the table. 'You – ,' he hisses. 'How did you get that costume?'

'I did a favour for Philip once,' pipes Motherwell, bending down to unlatch his uncomfortable spurs. 'I've done everybody a favour at one time or another, dear. Give a little, take a little, that's my motto. A ray of sunshine in everybody's life.'

Almost casually, Motherwell the Everlasting Executioner clips a magazine into his heavy Thompson sub-machine gun. He blazes a short and noisy burst at the chandeliers first, for practice, and the room suddenly tinkles with scintillating glass.

Then, his eyes metallic, he hammers at Retaud. The bullets bang into the table, very loudly, and Retaud scrambles away with the damask tablecloth around him, and his yelping dog getting caught under his feet.

Motherwell, thin and stooped, holds the gun up in his bony wrists and shoots again. The bullets tear after Retaud, starring mirrors, smashing glasses and plates, occasionally splattering into a guest. Long-legged Retaud scampers about the hall, sliding under tables, ducking and weaving and howling: 'STOP! STOP! I'M A FRIEND! I LOVE YOU! I ADORE YOU! ONLY STOP AND YOU CAN HAVE ME!'

'I wouldn't have you with corks in my ears and a rubber blindfold, honey,' says Motherwell, and shoots off another burst.

Finally, Retaud gets hopelessly tangled in the tablecloth, and lies on the floor, still shouting, trapped in the white soup-stained cocoon.

Motherwell prods him with his delicate ballet-dancer's toe. Then he inserts another magazine and fires into Retaud's jerking body until the tablecloth is bright red.

Silence falls. A waiter moves painstakingly round the hall, collecting up the dessert plates. Motherwell packs his weapon away and prepares to leave. Retaud's girl-friend Janine comes walking dazedly across, still in her corsets, and stares poached-egg eyes at him.

'What for?' she asks him, touching Retaud's blood-stained shroud with her bare foot. Her toes are streaked with gore.

Motherwell gives a bitter smile and shrugs. 'I haven't the faintest notion, ducks, but I'll give you thirty bob for that *agonising* corset.'

Fade out on Motherwell. Remember the last shroud. Almost casually, he vanishes into the chill evening chandeliers. Goodbye, Monsieur Retaud.

Reporter A14, thinly disguised as myself, moves after the Mysterious Babies on old time frequencies. The thin dust of the city settles like the wings of moths on the silent streets. His feet move in unknown directions, sensing out the radioactive patterns with Geiger toes. He takes his information from the scents of the dying hedgerow and the evening skyline of Earl's Court. He translates it into image blocks, three times faster than shorthand, best way of digesting the galactic schedules of the Mysterious Babies.

It is beginning to rain. The drops spot the windows and dapple the pavements. Reporter A14 puts up his coat collar and walks, head hunched, across Kensington Gore. A westbound Boeing thunders over the rustling trees. He smiles and lights a cigarette.

For your information the programme of Sliced Man. Mandrake the Magician peers out from behind a thousand corners. His face is lined and split, and shifts constantly from street to street. He whistles softly as he walks, and the dogs of London turn and prick up their ears to hear the strange electric message of dusk.

Remember the characters we are bringing into

play. Somewhere, behind the cardboard scenes of the city, Motherwell the Everlasting Programme walks with dusty feet around the joists and roof beams. J D Salinger, coughing agent of the western hills, peers out from behind the murky glass. 'He smiles and lights a cigarette.' Flash Gordon, remembering Brixton, sits with head in hands on a deserted doorstep. Dick Tracy and Junior whistle the dogs today the day.

Over the empty broken streets, a red white and blue kite. The National Anthem is being played in reverse by Johnson Willow, the music vendor of Charlotte Street. He has a magnificent collection of ancient and unknown instruments – plays to himself on a metal saw with a key file. The rich varnished bellies of his mandolins sway softly in the brown street. The thin strains of his music drift gently around, humming against frequencies of the Mysterious Babies. 'Life is but a dream … (peers out from behind a thousand corners).

Mysterious Music flows on trends of BABIES. Warbling in 'Charlotte Street' – shifting the keys of 'Kensington Gore'. Remember they move on harmonic schedules, touching the brow of the city from the mind's rim. Are you ready for Night Train – could almost feel Cold Sun. Are you ready for 'Tin Type Hall'?

Conversation taken from the notebooks of George Macfries, dead night editor of 'The Evening Mandolin', as interpreted by industrial reporter Ron Holland.

MACFRIES: I understand the dogs walk. Is that you?
TURNER: He smiles and lights a cigarette. A westbound Anthem follows the strange electric vendor of the rustling corners.
MACFRIES: Remember the characters we are

bringing into play.

TURNER: For your information the programme of Sliced Streets.

(There is hardly a breath of air in the heat. The trees are still and heavy with blood-red blossom. I walk slowly in the airless grass and stand under the shade of a coconut palm shading my eyes and looking out over the swampy inlet of Changi.)

He came out of the mud, an old man, his line clustered with cuttlefish, gray and wet from head to foot, his huge wide hat dripping and his feet leaving imprints on the track.

They passed on bicycles, ringing their bells and looking afraid of the dog. He smiled briefly, and lit a cigarette, a small black stub of tobacco that drifted fumes of fragrant forests across the snake grass.

And later that day, after the immediate sunset, I talked to a man under the flaring gaslight. At the oilcloth table, eating speedily with chopsticks, we talked about acupuncture and Chinese medicine.

'I take a live white mice, dip it in soy sauce, pull its tail off, and swallow it,' he grinned. 'Very good Chinese remedy for ulcers.'

Remember these characters we are bringing into play. The play in reverse. 'I take a live red kite'. He came out of the streets, gray and distant from strange electric message of dusk.

Reporter A14, in a white trench coat, armed with codebook based on three-dimensional mathematical progressions, hands glowing, arrives one rainy afternoon at the Woodside General Hospital. He drives his blue Anglia up the wet gravelled drive and parks at the door. The entrance is overgrown with ivy, and drips steadily under the silent gray sky.

He is driving along the wide carriageway towards Sutton when he notices a large Humber parked on the verge. A man is sitting at a small folding table with an airgun. He fires at passing cars, and records the hits on a scorecard. He is dressed in a red-and-white striped blazer, and straw hat, and wears round National Health glasses.

He gets out of the car and slams the door. The Woodside Hospital is quiet outside. Dismal trees surround it on every side, encroaching on the windows. The nearest sign of civilisation is the main London to Brighton railway cutting, dimly visible behind the leaves. A14 sniffs and pulls up his trench coat collar.

Inside the entrance hall it is dark and musty, and smells of hospital dinners. Today, butter beans and mince. There is a noise of squeaking wheels upstairs as a patient is rolled through the wards.

A14 (armed with codebook based on three-dimensional glass) taps at a small inquiry window. A white, withered face in a matron's cap looks up at him through the glass. He taps again, and the window slides back.

'Are you a visitor?' says the matron.

'No,' replies A14. He peers round in the darkness, hands in pockets. (He smiles and lights a cigarette).

The white matron says: 'If you're not a visitor, I'm afraid I must ask you to leave. This is a private hospital.'

A14 takes his miniature camera out of his coat and takes a flash photograph of the matron, then walks off into the darkness of the hall and up the stairs. He takes a flash photograph of a nude bronze statue on the banister rail. He takes a flash photograph of a passing nurse.

'Did you hear about the cannibal who passed his friend in the street?'

'Just telling you today – today, butter, beans and mince.'

He walks quickly along the linoleum corridor. The walls are painted a dull hospital brown. He passes the sterilising room, where a group of chattering nurses are brewing tea in the scalpel boiler. They stare at A14 and he snaps a picture of them.

'I'm so depressed. I don't know which way to turn. My life is a dead-end. There's nothing I can do. I can no longer think in logical terms. I can no longer think of anything. I can't remember what my child looks like. I don't know which way to turn. I'm so depressed. There's nothing I can do.'

'Quiet, please. Just telling you he walks quickly along the electric corridor.'

Further along the carriageway, he sees a man in swimming trunks standing on an overpass bridge. The man is wearing huge feathered wings. The gale flutters them, and the man's face is turned to the sky. He zooms on, past the gas station, past the AA centre, past the thundery clouds and the poplars turning their silver backs to the wind.

'This way, please. Doctor Cary will see you in just a moment.'

A14 sits down on a hard steel-and-canvas chair in the gloomy corridor, next to five other patients. Two of them are reading primeval copies of *Woman's Own*. The other three stare blankly at the opposite wall. There is a scratch on a nearby radiator in the shape of a dachshund.

A14's face melts and shifts. He no longer looks like me, but his gestures and his voice betray him. He takes photographs of the little line of patients and then sits down again, with his legs crossed. One of the patients, an elderly woman in spectacles, stares at him balefully. She doesn't even look away when he stares back.

He looks down at his shoes. They are worn and scuffed. The lino under them is chipped and dirty. He rubs his hands wearily on his face.

In the seat beside him is a very young girl, not more than 12, and yet already very poised and pretty. She has a thin face, eyes thick and sooty with make-up, and long, almost colourless hair. Tiny breasts under a scorched school blouse. A ring on her pale finger, a gold Scottie dog with a green glass eye.

'It's horrible weather, isn't it?' says A14 to the girl. She turns to him, not sure if he's speaking to her, and he can see her eyes are faded blue.

(The same colour as the dress she had when she was six, and very small. In a vivid field of red and green poppies, under a sky of ceramic purple and creamy clouds, a tiny dot of blue, moving from flower to flower, each one more exciting than the last.)

'Yes,' she says, even though they're not really talking about the weather at all, nobody ever does.

'I suppose you've had a day off school to come here,' comments A14. He feels old and grubby in his trench coat.

'Yes, I had to. I might have to have an operation.'

A14 frowns at her. 'Will it be very serious?'

'I'm not really sure,' she replies quietly, shifting her hair with her thin fingers. 'It was after I fell off the garage roof looking for apples.'

(She is lying quite still. A fly touches her blue-veined eyelid and wipes its proboscis watchfully. There is a scent of damp green grass and rotting apples. Her dress is white. She seems to be sinking in the weeds.)

'Which school do you go to?'

'Kensington High School for Girls. I'm in the second form. I take my GCEs the year after the year after next. I'm taking six subjects.'

A14 smiles briefly. He doesn't feel like smiling. Seeing this girl in this dim dirty corridor of the hospital makes him sad and depressed. He fishes out his cigarettes but the packet is empty. He crushes it in his hand and drops it on the floor.

'Do you want a cigarette?' asks the girl. A14 looks at her blankly. She reaches down to her black plastic handbag and takes out a packet of 10 Nelson.

'You shouldn't smoke, you know,' grins A14 as he takes one. But what worries him more is stealing her cigarettes. He lights it carefully and blows smoke across the corridor.

'I don't do it often,' she says. 'This is only the second packet I've ever bought. I got them to smoke on the train, but I don't really like them very much. I watch myself smoking in the mirror.'

'Do the other girls smoke? At school, I mean?'

'No, only a few of the grown-up ones. Not many of the girls in my class are very mature. They're like junior school children. Avril Spain still draws spikes round the sun, and a face on it. I was the only one who was wearing a brassiere in the juniors. Most of the other girls are still like beanpoles. They get absolutely scandalised if you wear frilly knickers or anything like that. Miss Harpole – she's our gym mistress – says we've all got to wear those terrible navy-blue serge ones that come up to your chin. I got detention eleven times last year.'

(Sitting at old battered desk in the classroom as the sun slides orange along the wall. The bowed head of the teacher marking books. The restless child with her white socks round her ankles and scuffed shoes, dreaming away detention with drawings of hills and palaces and jutting-jawed heroes.)

'What subjects do you like best?' asks A14. He whips out his camera and takes a flash picture of a passing doctor.

'English and chemistry, because we have Mrs Myerscough for chemistry. We call her the Microscope.' She pauses. 'Why do you keep taking pictures?'

A14 smiles again. 'It's my job. I take hundreds of pictures in the course of the day, and file them all. They're very useful to me.'

'I took a photograph with Mummy's camera once, of a friend of mine and her pony. But it didn't come out. I didn't hold it still enough.'

'Why aren't your parents here today?' I ask the girl.

She shakes her head. 'They're abroad at the moment. I board at the school – me and another girl, Christine Moritz. We have to stay there all through the holidays, but sometimes we go on visits to the Natural History Museum and places like that. We saw Buffy Sainte-Marie once, but the head didn't approve. She thinks we ought to spend every evening listening to (Mozart, Berlioz, Wagner) in her terrible old study. We go to tea with the head sometimes. She has walnut cake, and we have to have milk, because tea will keep us awake, and we might dream of gorgeous boys or something.'

A14 has an urge to kiss the girl. Just to comfort her, although she doesn't need comforting. He doesn't really know what she needs. She seems devastatingly lonely, and yet she's so bright and cheerful. Perhaps he wants to kiss her because she attracts him. He finishes his cigarette and grinds it out.

He says: 'What do you suppose – ', but just then a nurse leans round the door and beckons to the girl. She picks up her handbag and her magazine and smiles at him, then follows the nurse into the room. The door shuts, and A14 is left with the four aged patients and the rain beating against the grimy windows.

I have visions of taking the girl for walks through Hyde Park on a hot day. She's wearing a pink-and-white gingham dress, and I can almost hear the sound of her laugh. We stop to look in the windows of shops along Park Lane, and she's got her arm unconsciously in mine, so that people mistake us for father and daughter.

Or even into a night-club – she in a shiny black evening dress with a white flower in her breast – her hair up and expensive earrings glittering on her neck. The smooth sound of the orchestra and the waiter saying: 'This way, please'.

'She thinks we ought to spend every evening listening to (Turner, Motherwell, George Macfries)'

'Just telling you this is all a mistake.'

'It was a bet. We were seeing how many distinguished flowers we could smooth into the cigarette. The door shuts and the devastatingly lonely sound of electric wires.'

Yes, the impossible times we could have. Humbert A14 Humbert and his boarding-school Lolita (haring through Trafalgar Square on a grainy day, with the pigeons bursting like shrapnel all around us). I buy her a 6d tin of birdseed, and they flutter all over her, and my camera freezes her laugh, and I find the snapshot later in the back of my wallet, torn and grubby, and stare at it as the rain pours like blood down the windows of the Woodside Hospital.

FLASHBACK TO HAYMARKET: And the dark agents of Tin Type Hall have hit Jack Beauregard. He crawls bleeding across the pavement, humping himself for shelter in a shop doorway. His fingernails scratch at the concrete like a turtle heaving itself down the beach. The quiet whistle of pistols with silencers – and he is hit again. A purple splash on the side of his head, as though a plum has been squashed against it. The day all around is silent.

Time film of Dr Cary the old surgeon. Dr Cary the only man who can approach Tin Type Hall. Now sitting in the washroom after the operation drinking neat gin out of a grimy tumbler. He lights a cigarette and steadies his shaking hands.

'I resent your intrusion,' he says in his ghostly voice as A14 enters, a hard look in his eyes. A14 takes a flash photograph of him and leaves the room.

Or in an aged Ford Zephyr, driving through bad weather up the A1, she's sitting beside me reading comics and eating After Eight mints (I pamper them with wafer-thin pistols), and we turn off at Fortes for a cup of weak coffee and an orange juice on the chilly Formica tables.

She says: 'It's a great adventure, isn't it?'

A14 keeps a lookout for the dark agents of Tin Type Hall. Dr Cary peers out from behind a thousand corners. Just telling you we turn off the operation. A purple splash of gin in the shaking doorway. Or in an aged pistol, I resent your photograph. The quiet whistle of 'Drop in sometime.'

A rusty clock at the end of the corridor strikes (Mozart, Berlioz, Wagner). The door of the operating theatre opens. Two male nurses with brawny arms emerge, carefully leading a wheelchair.

She's sitting in it (as you might have guessed) with a tartan blanket around her knees. Her spine looks crooked, and her thin white hand with the golden Scottie dog ring is clasped against her throat. Her eyes are vacant, and her mouth is hanging open in a terrible imbecilic expression.

A14 sits on his iron chair with quiet dread soaking his feet. The nurses (smell of medical alcohol and perspiration) roll the chair past the waiting patients. The cretinous girl doesn't even look at him as she is taken past. He snaps a photograph of her (Eddie Constantine peers out from behind a thousand corners) and the day fragments into glass.

'What have you done?' he shouts to Dr Cary in the cavernous washroom. The cisterns are gurgling so that he can hardly hear.

Dr Cary takes another drink: and shakes his head drunkenly. He whispers: 'It's the *Hypocritic Oath*, old boy. Everything possible was done to save her.'

The intrepid two are faced with foul, fearsome, fiendish folly in the horrible hand of the Rotten Rhymer. A Bluenite Bomb! (Well may you boggle!) If the Rhymer succeeds with his diabolical plan he will clean up!

CRUMP! Blecht and curses, the bomb went bang, but caused no chaos, what went wrang? ... er ... wrong!

Tough custard, Rhymer! I used my atomic powered Batair Cleeny Weeny Wick! Puts a full Nelson on fall-out and 3d off at all good supermarkets!

Quite like Mother Murfies Tinned Chicken there is nothing – The only chicken with the less fattening stuffing!

'Everything possible, old boy, was done to save her. I assure you we tried every medical facility at our disposal. There was absolutely no other way out of it.'

(A14 is screaming out loud now, but he can hear nothing. He is shaking the Dr's thin withered throat in its soft collar, but the Dr is no longer inhabiting the body. He is standing washing his hands by the basin and talking to me over his shoulder.)

'Your demand for positive proof – just let me get this mud off my hands – will be met, Mr Crisp. I will take you to the operating theatre personally. Have you seen a towel anywhere?'

(THE OPERATING THEATRE: We need not spend long here. It is all recorded on photographs. Most of them are clear, but there are a few missing. The light wasn't good, you must remember. They are not in the right order, either.)

Twenty identical girls, each drooling quietly on to school blouse, sit on narrow benches in the corridor. They stare blankly into space, making a murmuring sound or disjointed phrases. A14 walks up the row, inspecting on the hand of each girl a golden Scottie ring with a green glass eye.

'Forsooth, and fivesooth, even!' cries Dr Cary. The dark agents of Tin Type Hall (Mozart, Berlioz, Wagner) stand in the shadows of the hospital with their silencers. A14 already running towards them waving his hands, but changes his mind and dives for the floor, pulling his revolver from its shoulder holster, and scrambling back to a doorway.

(Everybody in this book is armed. Many of the characters have been recruited from an unfinished film 'Billy the Kid', started in 1910. They were loath to give up their weapons – and most of them did not want to give up the plot of the movie they had been working on for so long. This accounts for the gunplay, and the strange silvery faces of the characters, which you may have noticed.)

2
hi-ho, etc.

Technical analysis of fragments of the Programme of Sliced Man, discovered by Immodesty Blaze, our female trouble-shooter from Wandsworth, indicate that some sort of attempt is going to be made on the life of Jack Beauregard, the Eater of Cities.

Jack Beauregard is in an invidious position as far as Tin Type Hall is concerned. He is a long-time friend of Envoy John, otherwise known as Starving Eamonn Midnight, the man who leaked 400 confidential Tin Type Hall documents to The Evening Trousers.

(All this is quite spurious, of course. We have to present a cover-story for the benefit of our publisher and reporters. The fragments were actually found in a taxi parked outside Euston Station on March 4, 1966.)

Immodesty Blaze, cardboard female character, dressed in black tights and with a leather gun belt strung at her side, enters the office with her assistant, lovable Cockney Willie Garlic, played here by our old contact William Turner.

'I climbed the fire escape at the back of Tin Type

Hall, killed the guards with my high-power catapult, blew open the safe and escaped with these,' she says, arching a meticulously-plucked eyebrow.

William Turner is drunk on Napoleon brandy, and keeps forgetting to adopt a Cockney accent. White and breathless, he sits on a chair in the corner of the office and lights a Gauloise. He coughs and titters from time to time.

Immodesty Blaze, forty-inch breasts like rockets, cartoon splodge for a mouth, folds herself into a seat and waits for our reply. I call the Night Editor, George Macfries, and show him the fragments.

They are quite tiny – frail, skeleton-leaf, pieces. In a few of them you can just make out the traces of pound-note metal used as radioactive schedules for the computers of Tin Type Hall.

I pick up the phone and ask for the Director of Tin Type Hall. They put me through to the water-rate department instead, and there is a confused muttering of voices, like a dying crowd scene.

'Is that you?' I say down the telephone.

'Just telling you all lines are blocked. The electric death shifts over the city. It is impossible to contact the last word of the power station.'

'He claimed that sea was imbalance between "short and sweet",' I reply. 'He agreed that once fence chiefs over the journal. The strike started two days ago – biggest illusion since the country would drag on for Indian rope trick.'

Headline for today: JACK BEAUREGARD FEARS FOR LIFE. Police guard for his Sutton home. By Special Co-respondent, Wilfred Shoes.

'Analyse these pieces,' snaps George, and disappears down the office corridor, leaving a smell of pink cigars and wilting rose petals.

'Come on, Willie, we've got to smash the Magnus gang,' says Immodesty Blaze harshly. She gets up to leave, but the 90 minutes has run out, and she fades into old silver cover-story. Her hands dissolve from the door and she flickers into time-film afternoon.

'And I'll follow your casket – in the pale afternoon,' sings Bob Dylan fan Prince Albert from his rusty perch. He sighs as traffic passes through Kensington Gore, not giving him a second glance. He says: 'I'm no longer a prince – I'm a fixture.'

The Programme of Sliced Man, as far as our laboratories can determine, is based on the principle of eidetics. This involves the afterimage produced on the eye and the brain by strong stimulation. It enables one to investigate and describe a picture that is no longer before the eye.

Simply, an after-image is produced by the 'fatiguing' of the appropriate part of the retina after continued stimulation by a particular source. Interesting side-effects are that the 'image' produced covers an area directly proportional to the distance of the surface on which the eye perceives it.

John Remorse, Agent One Section Three, also known as The Serjeant of Time Film, is operating the Eidetic Scheme for Tin Type Hall. His last assignment was in Kuwait, where he produced afterimages of oil derricks while the real ones were dismantled and smuggled out of Arabia by the Egyptians.

(Hot morning in Kuwait. A fresh breeze blows in from the Persian Gulf on to the flat sand. The black smoke of oil fires marks the horizon. In the makeshift airport, we are sitting drinking watery instant coffee. The aircraft outside ripples in the heat from the runway. There is a smell of kerosene and Arabia.)

'The strength of my afterimages is such,' explains John Remorse, poking at the sugar with his spoon, 'that an Arab mechanic actually climbed one of the illusory oil derricks, adjusted a ring with his spanner, and climbed down again.'

Master of Time, Film and Eidetics, he was born in Hampshire, and was head boy at Winchester College. He trained as a water dowser, but was ejected from the fellowship after an incident on Box Hill, when his hazel twig went berserk and tried to rape a nearby police constable.

> JUDGE: It is – eh – not so much the fact that – eh – the said twig attempted an assault of an – eh – unsavoury nature on an officer of the law, which is – eh – in itself an offence of the gravest nature, but – eh – the fact that it was a male that the – eh – said twig went for. Had it been an – eh – attractive young member of the – eh – opposite sex, its behaviour might have been excusable. But if there is – eh – one thing that this Court will not tolerate, it is a – eh – QUEER TWIG.'

John Remorse grew a moustache and went to work for the Chinese Government. There was a photograph of him in the Evening News, standing just behind Mao-Tse-Tung. He was recognised by our reporters and a foreign correspondent sent to interview him.

'What the Chinese wanted,' John explained, sitting on the veranda of his house, throwing salted black olives to the monkeys in his garden, 'was a dangerous situation that would discredit the United States and Britain.'

He smiled and lit a cigarette. 'I produced one of my most effective eidetic images yet. We removed Indo-China, leaving a replacement image behind, and transported it to Mongolia, where we still have it.

'This makes me positive that the Vietnam War cannot last. Within a year or so, the image will fade, and both Americans and Vietnamese will find they are swimming about in the South China Sea. Can you beat that?'

'Very droll,' says George Macfries, pouring himself a mug of tea from the office urn. 'I want the stories by tonight – for the West End Final if you can do it. Nail down Remorse and show up the Sliced Man Programme for what it is.'

This makes me positive that the strength of my after-images is a confused muttering of schedules. He smiled and grew a moustache. Master of Fragments and Taxi, he climbed the fire-escape and fades into technical analysis. I'll follow your casket – drop in sometime. We've got to smash the Indian rope trick.

He claimed that sea was old silver cover-story. A fresh breeze blows in Chinese illusion. One thing that this Photograph will not tolerate. Remember the mind's agent. (Motherwell, Turner, Macfries).

This is the after-image produced on the side-effects by smuggled situation. As far as our laboratories can determine, Agent Oil Section Brain is last assignment. Its behaviour might have been excusable. Just telling you the Mysterious Babies burnt the varnish of the night's mutterings.

So here we are as evening falls in Hill Street, in the backwaters of Soho. It's a narrow street, and the smell of Italian cooking lingers under the dim green lights. In the lighted window of El Mapa Restaurant, you can see a crowd of Greeks lounging and smoking and drinking espresso coffee. An occasional car creeps down the street, driven by a tired teenager in a pink blazer. It's Saturday night, in case you hadn't noticed, and the hot dog vendor on the corner vanishes from time to time in a cloud of steam.

Samuel Baptist gets out of his juddering taxi at the end of the street and pays the driver. The cabbie stares down at the tip as though a bird has shit in his hand.

'I could let you 'ave the whole bleeding taxi for this, mate,' he shouts. But Samuel waves him away, and walks down the street in a cloud of expensive aftershave and cigar smoke.

He pushes through the wandering crowds until he reaches a dark, narrow doorway. He looks up it, tapping his teeth with his cane, and then strides in.

Up a murky flight of stairs, an evil-smelling old woman with nicotine-stained hair is sitting at a table listening to Radio London. Behind her is a plastic ribbon curtain, through which can be heard the sound of voices and laughter.

'Good evening,' grins Samuel, bowing slightly. 'Is the proprietor about?'

'The what, friend?' quavers the old woman, cupping her hand to her ear. 'Speak up a bit, carn 'ear yer.'

'The proprietor. The manager,' repeats Samuel patiently.

The old woman rubs her bearded chin for a moment, then turns in her chair and bawls out: 'Mrs Binfield! Yer wanted!'

Samuel leans against the banisters, humming

selections from 'White Horse Inn'. He grinds his cigar out under his elegant shoe, smiles at the old lady, who scowls back, and adjusts his tie.

Finally the plastic curtain parts with a rattle. Mrs Binfield, a heavy-jawed woman of at least 50, thickly made up and wearing a skin-tight snakeskin dress, gushes out onto the landing.

'How do you do, sir,' she says, exposing four layers of lipstick-tinged dentures. 'Hai hope my secretahry 'as made you welcome.'

'Abundantly, madam,' replies Samuel. 'Perhaps we could go inside.'

With a fluttering laugh, Mrs Binfield leads the way through the curtain. We are now in a large shabby sitting-room, with a worn brown carpet and dilapidated furniture. Mrs Binfield flits from chair to chair, beating up clouds of dust from each one. She motions Samuel to sit down, and perches herself on the edge of the sofa.

'We aim to please, sir,' she says, fanning herself with a tattered copy of Dalton's Weekly.

'I sincerely hope so,' says Samuel smoothly. He looks briefly round the room, sniffing dry-rot and stale cigarette smoke. The lamp on the table is made out of a Dimple Whisky bottle, and the table itself is supported by a copy of Pear's Cyclopaedia.

'I have an album, with full details of the young ladies, if you so desire to 'ave a look at it, sir,' coos Mrs Binfield.

'Yes,' says Samuel. 'I shall need that. How many rooms have you?'

'Ho, habout eight, sir. Not including the littlest, sir, if you see what I mean, ha-ha,' she answers.

'Good,' says Samuel. He flicks quickly through

the album, stopping now and then to frown at alleged vital statistics of 45 and over, and then drops it on the table. 'Right, let's go.'

'Go?' queries Mrs Binfield, a little puzzled. 'You 'aven't yet specified, sir, which of the young ladies took your fancy.'

Samuel lowers his dark eyebrows. 'All of them,' he says. 'I want them all. Down here, right away.'

The corner of Mrs Binfield's mouth sags. She bites her lip. Then she leans forward and says in a confidential whisper: 'Are you sure, sir? I mean, are you quite up to it? There's six of them, you know.'

'Splendid, splendid,' replies Samuel softly. 'And if they're not busy at the moment, I would like to have them down here.'

Mrs Binfield, as if in a dream, staggers over to the foot of the stairs. She rings a discreet little bell, to inform any gentleman upstairs that there is a gentleman downstairs whom he may not wish to encounter, and then walks slowly up. She gives Samuel a last bewildered look.

Selections from 'White Horse Inn'. And then a heavy noise of seven pairs of feet coming downstairs. Samuel has a brief mental joke of Snow White and the Seven Dwarfs. Then he stands up to greet the girls.

'These are Vera, Susan, Lydia, Violet, Storme and Patricia,' announces Mrs Binfield. She has by now regained her composure, and is rubbing her hands and swaggering in a professional way.

The girls crowd in the corner of the room, staring sullenly at Samuel and saying nothing. He smiles politely, and then ushers them into an untidy line with his cane.

Samuel paces back and forth, inspecting the girls

closely. They are all short and heavily proportioned, and they have rings under their eyes like plums.

Vera, mature and dark-haired, is dressed in a thick blue-flannel dressing gown. Susan and Lydia are both in transparent baby-doll nightdresses, Lydia without knickers. Violet, Storme and Patricia are wearing shapeless suits.

'Is Storme your real name?' Samuel asks her suavely.

'Yes, actually, if you must know,' snaps the girl. 'I was born in a bloody Post Office in the middle of a thunderstorm. I don't wonder me parents didn't put a bloody stamp on me and call me parcelleta.'

Mrs Binfield clucks about behind Samuel, peering over his shoulder, and occasionally adjusting one of the girls' earrings or hair. She frowns disapprovingly at knickerless Lydia.

Samuel sits himself on the arm of a chair and faces the girls. He says: 'I expect you're wondering why I want you all and who I am.'

'All right, six-shot Tex, who are yer?' says Storme.

Samuel sniffs delicately at his carnation buttonhole. 'I am Samuel Baptist,' he says. 'Her Majesties' Inspector of Brothels.'

Mrs Binfield sits down with relief. She fans herself with a brassiere and gasps. 'For a moment, you know,' she flutters, 'I thought you were from Egon Ronay. All I've got is a tin of Heinz Spaghetti and a bit of Cheddar.'

Samuel allows himself a little smile. Then he takes a large dossier out his pocket and opens it up. He unscrews a gold propelling pencil and makes a few preparatory notes.

'I shall have to ask you a few questions, of

course,' he says. I have some associates arriving later with the test equipment itself. Now tell me, what are your hours?'

'Monday to Saturday from 6:30pm to 4:00 AM, early closing on Wednesdays,' says Mrs Binfield.

'What tastes can you cater for? Do you have adequate equipment?'

'Quite a fair little wardrobe, sir. Our latest addition is an Arabian camel-whip. You pull the handle and there's a tempered steel spike in it.'

The question and answer session continues for over half an hour. Then there is the sound of feet on the stairs, and voices saying 'Steady with her', and 'Your end up a bit.'

Through the plastic curtain come the Famous Ear and Workman Bill, sweating profusely and dressed in grimy overalls. Between them they are carrying a large machine, not unlike an automatic washing-machine.

'Got anywhere I can plug it in?' Workman Bill asks loudly. He takes a puff at his cigarette stub and scratches himself.

They switch on the machine. Samuel leads the girls towards it and indicates that they should stand in a little ring.

'This is a libido tester,' explains Samuel. 'It shows us how efficient you are at your job, and whether your productivity is on a par with Government requirements.'

'In other words,' interrupts the Famous Ear, 'what we wants to know is – are we getting enuff bangs out of yer for our money?'

Samuel twirls a dial, and the white machine starts humming loudly. It vibrates, and the vibrations make it creep sideways across the faded carpet. The faces of the girls watch it, fascinated.

After a few seconds, Samuel bends down to inspect the meter reading. He registers surprise, and beckons the Famous Ear over to his side stop. The girls peer over at him, trying to see if anything is wrong.

The Famous Ear adjusts the switch, but still Samuel looks puzzled. Finally he walks quickly over to Mrs Binfield and says: 'Is there another girl in the house?'

Mrs Binfield flaps her hands about distraught. 'Of course not sir, these are all I've got. We used to have a seventh, Muriel, a heavy girl, sir. A very hard worker, but it weren't no good for the beds. One night two years ago, she and her sailor pal from the HMS. Outrageous fell right through the springs and into the restaurant downstairs. A good girl, sir, but she's gone now, rest her soul.'

Samuel lights another cigar and does some pacing. (Selections from 'White Horse Inn'). He bites his thumbnail anxiously. Then he snatches up his cane and walks around the furniture, prodding it.

As he reaches the sofa, the springs under the shabby upholstery begin to ripple. Samuel leans over it more closely, and begins sticking his cane into it even more. The sofa seems to shudder and recoil like a living thing. Its springs twang in unison and chorus, and its wheels squeak excitedly on the carpet.

The Famous Ear says: 'Bloody hell.'

Samuel nods at him grimly, and repeatedly shoves his stick into the sofa, doing it rhythmically and with increasing speed. The air in the stuffy sitting room becomes charged with strange electric waves. Unseen messages warble from distant wires. The girls stand well back, their eyes bulging in amazement.

The poking gets faster and faster, and Samuel is sweating. The livid brown sofa seems to pant clouds of dust. It shifts and moves like frames from an ancient film. Just telling you this is out to smash the Indian rope trick.

Harder and harder works Samuel, now digging the cane deep into the cushions. There is an invisible high-pitched whine in the room that escapes their eyes and pierces their ears. The dense, sultry charge of electricity builds up in strange condensers.

Without warning, the sofa jerks as if hit by a sledgehammer. The material at the back splits open, and a mass of black horsehair bulges out on to the floor. Then, with a final shudder, the sofa lies empty and sated.

It's the message, you see, that has reached us at the dying offices of the Evening Cuffs. It's typed on thin fawn official paper, and headed with a Government crest. It arrives on my desk as the Late Extra is going to bed.

'Is that you?'

'Just telling you there is only a cover charge. Drop in sometime.'

The story of Jack Beauregard, the Eater of Cities. I refuse to say where he was born; after all it would only be a name. His father (Reginald Beauregard, Senior, a mild man with watery eyes and few interests) was quietly wasting his life away in a small bicycle business in Harrow. He made most of his small income selling inner tubes to young married couples. His mother, Dolores Beauregard, nee Beauregard, only married him because he had the same name, and she had a passion for names. She carried a grubby exercise-book with her, noting down in her slow, heavy hand, any name that interested her. She would repeat a name over and over, until it no longer gave her any satisfaction. 'It's chewed dry now,' she used to say, 'like a juicy grass stem.'

Her sexual relationships with Reginald Beauregard were reduced practically to nil by the time Jack had reached (Spock, Luria, Krafft-Ebbing). Her sole function was to provide her husband with mince and baked beans and HP sauce (Harold Wilson's favourite) once a day. Then she would sit by the window, stirring the yellowed lace curtains, staring out over the dusty Harrow side road, and whispering over and over: 'Amersham … Amersham …' with a soft slur and a vibrant hum on the m's.

FLASHBACK TO HAYMARKET: They've hit him, they've hit your boy. They've shot him in face and stomach and groin. He's lying there glassy-eyed with a purple bubble in his lips, whispering with you now. The dark agents have smashed your son like a pulpy orange, and he's lying there as the invisible crowds in white step over his body.

At school, Jack Beauregard formed a close and slightly unhealthy relationship with a geography master called Killick, or Cullip. Killick-Cullip was unmarried, 50ish, with a thin chicken-like neck and an overpowering nose. He sat in a permanent aura of chalk-dust and mouldy underpants, the Harrow sun perching on his nose. The red veins alight like an embryo chick inside a phosphorescent egg. You got the feeling that if the sun was warm enough, floating black eyes and a transparent beak would develop inside his nose, and finally hatch.

A faded photograph of the young Jack Beauregard shows him as lanky youth, with thick artery-filled hands, and an unusually small head. He is standing next to a tree (probably an oak) which has the sign 'DEER MUST NOT BE SHOT EXCEPT WITH SPECIAL PERMISSION, See The Head Warden, Mr R Grisling.'

And a moment after that photograph was taken, Killick or Cullip put down his camera, and said in a thin voice: 'I wouldn't shoot you, dear, even if I did have special permission.'

It is hard to estimate what influence the geography master had on the growing Jack. There were teas (it is rumoured) at Killick or Cullip's seedy flat, not far from the school gates. There were (in a whisper) breakfasts. But at no time were there any overt homosexual actions between the two.

'In his flat, he would gently unbutton my trousers, and fondle me. There was always a smell of chalk from the school, and the greasy remains of our sickening tea lay around on chairs and on the floor. He had a picture of his mother, or someone else's mother, on the mantelpiece. Next to it was one of those striped glass tubes of coloured sand from the Isle of Wight.

'"What is produced by the Norwegians in the Stavanger region?" he would ask me, nuzzling that great waxy nose of his in my pubic curls. I would look down at him, and there was dandruff in his parting, and say without hesitation: "Herring"'

(Beverley Nichols and Somerset Maugham talking on a hot evening. Beverley Nichols stares into Maugham's eroded eyes and points his finger at the old writer's nose. A naked man is lying upstairs under a heap of Maugham's novels, laughing loudly and reading passages from 'Cakes and Ale'. It's hotter than the day before, and the cicadas are whirring loudly.)

The Captain of Kodak peers out from behind a thousand corners and records the life of Jack Beauregard the Eater of Cities. The wires are buzzing today the day. Stirring the yellowed remains, and whispering over and over: 'Invisible … invisible …' Just telling you the long sad story of Jack Beauregard the Eater of Breakfasts, sole function like a juicy grass stem.

What happens next is uncertain. There is an indication that the relationship was broken off. A girl's name is mentioned. A fat girl, pale and spotted with acne. Killick or Cullip is saying something in a desperate whine, but it is hard to make out his words. There is something about 'infidelity' and 'herrings', but we can conclude nothing from these isolated fragments.

Jack Beauregard entered the College of Aeronautical Engineers at Chelsea in 1923. His name appears on the ledgers in a backward-sloping handwriting in mauve marking ink. It is more faded than the others, and less mature.

(Also in the ledger, by purest coincidence, the name of George Macfries, night editor of the Evening Valise, who took a three-year course in aero-engine maintenance. He was later to be involved with William Turner and other unidentified parties in a series of fatal accidents.)

'They're after me,' wrote Jack Beauregard in 1947. 'They're all around me, I can feel them. They're laying their traps out there and they mean to get me. There's no way of stopping them. They're everywhere, they're watching me, and there's nothing I can do.'

He was at that time, according to his closest friend, photographer Gordon Caspar, 'an isolated ... guilty-looking young man. He would sidle about the corridors of the college ... with his head on one side and a grimace of fear on his face ...'

(We see him now as a member of the Chelsea Flounderers Boating Crew. He is wearing a tweed cap, and it is hard to see his face. He is peering across the water as if on the lookout. It was later discovered that he carried a shotgun in his boating bag.)

CASPAR: An isolated ... unidentified fear. He was later to make out in a desperate whine. He is wearing a fatal ledger.
BEAUREGARD: Everybody knows and he's already as good as finished.

(So floating lazily back to shore on the flow tide, it's only slight here on the backing Equator, just enough to stir the thick white blossom that drifts about my face and crowns me with white.)

Jack Beauregard then took to drawing. He bought a packet of children's crayons and an exercise book from a local newsagent, and sat in his room overlooking the Underground line where it emerges at West Kensington. He spent hours producing crude, multi-coloured sketches of the houses and the trains that he could see from his tiny window.

LANDLADY: 'E drew lovely, you know. I never saw anyone draw as good as what 'e did. Some of 'is colours looked good enough to eat.

(Eat? We forget the reputation. Jack Beauregard the Last Agent of Tin Type Hall. Jack Beauregard the Eater of Cities. Strange suburbs dissolve under his cold grasp. His hard eyes under his hair look out from the deserted cafes and corners of Streatham.)

> CRISP: You were an agent for Tin Type Hall.
> BEAUREGARD: I was not an agent. I have never worked for them. I know nothing about it whatsoever.
> CRISP: But they are after you.
> BEAUREGARD: Yes, they are after me. I can see no way at the present tide (sic) of getting away. I shall just have to sit and wait.
> CRISP: What is your story?

The story of Jack Beauregard, the Eater of Cities. Have you seen Manchester? Have you seen Cardiff? Who was responsible for the Second World War? ('I was wounded in the buttocks at Monte Cassino. I had a bloody gorgeous time in that little Italian town, recuperating.') Where is Brixton? Where is Los Angeles? Where are Buffalo and Winchester and Canterbury?

The Captain of Kodak appears in the office doorway and beckons me over. He tears open an envelope and smiles. He tips it up, and a stream of black paper ash drifts to the floor. He is not smiling any more, just staring at the ash.

'The Mysterious Babies –'

'Just telling you this is the last dream of Jack Beauregard.'

A new way of committing suicide. Fill your nostrils with plastic explosive, and wire the explosive to your electric clock. Go to bed, and try to get to sleep. You can always breathe through your mouth. At 7.30 in the morning, your wife will come in with your morning cup of tea, and you will blow up with a magnificent noise, and the bedroom will have to be redecorated.

'I am so depressed. I don't know which way to turn. I can't feel anything anymore. It's hopeless trying to find a way out. There is no solution, no answer to any of my problems. They're insurmountable. There's absolutely no way out …'

Reporter A14, his disguise showing signs of wear, walks through the busy morning light of Earl's Court Road, screwing up his eyes against the Sun.

It is too early for most people to be about, so we have used for this scene a number of stock extras. A14 pushes his way past Mandrake the Magician, Immodesty Blaze, William Turner, Nubar Gulbenkian, Marcello Mastroianni, Tiffany Jones and Teddy and the Pirates. They smile at him as he passes, and their smiles fade in the bright 6:00 AM glare.

He has an appointment for breakfast with Samuel Baptist, HM Inspector of Brothels, and Charlie Bowdre, organiser of the Original Victorian Naughties. A note from George Macfries indicates that they have some new project in hand.

('Took him his tea, I did. Then the alarm clock goes off and there's a bloody great bang and he's sitting on the TV aerial in his pyjamas with a terrible nosebleed. Well, that's one way to get you up in the bloody morning, I says. We couldn't watch Hughie Green for about six weeks because the silly fool had bent the aerial.')

Charlie Bowdre has a flat in Grosvenor Square, in the vast early morning shadow of the American Embassy. There are two Rolls-Royces parked outside under the trees as I walk up to the door.

I knock, chafing my hands together. After a few minutes, there is a buzz from a speaker beside the door, and a female voice says: 'Who's that knocking?'

(It's only me from over the sea, A14 the Aerial.)

There is a pause, and then the door clicks open automatically. I push it open, and step carefully into the wide, luxurious hallway. There is a heavy scent of orchids and hairspray, like the foyer of a women's hairdresser.

'This way, please,' says a brittle voice. A woman (I hadn't seen her) steps out from behind a spray of narcissus and beckons me. She is dull blonde, attractive in a solid-featured way, but with legs like a well-turned dinner table.

She takes my old fawn raincoat and leads the way up a hushed flight of stairs. When we reach the double doors of Charlie Bowdre's flat, she opens them and nods to me to go in.

The blinds are still closed in the flat, and the fluorescent lights are on. Charlie Bowdre, in an exotic red smoking jacket, is lounging back in an armchair with a brandy glass in his hand. Samuel Baptist, immaculately dark-suited and smelling of aftershave, is browsing through the vast leather-bound library of erotica.

'Ah, the Press,' says Bowdre, in the same tone as a man saying: 'Ah, a heap of shit.' He waves casually as A14 stalks cautiously in. 'I say Samuel, the Press.'

'Good egg,' replies Baptist, without looking up.

Bowdre is a small chimpanzee of a man, with a violent gingery moustache. His face looks on the point of explosion any moment, and something dry and wrinkled might flop out if it did. He bangs languidly at a gong, and smiles at A14, but says nothing.

A girl appears from an invisible door. In fact there is no door, but the girl appears.

She is small, young and dark. She is wearing nothing but a man's white vest, inside out, so that the red label shows. Her neck moves shyly in a graceful swallowing motion.

With a timid grin, the girl sits on the arm of Bowdre's chair and poses. The nest of hairs between her thighs is blue-black and shiny.

'This,' says Bowdre brightly, moving aside the girl's right breast with his hand to get a better view of me, 'is my latest invention.'

'I see,' I reply quietly, sitting down in an overstuffed leather chair and lighting a Churchman's tipped cigarette. 'It's gorgeous. But hasn't it been invented before?'

Bowdre grins, and shoves his hairy little hand between the girl's plump legs. 'Yes, friend, in a way. But not the way I'm going to do it. Not on your life, boy.'

The girl has a semi-Oriental look about her. She smiles at me vaguely, unaware Bowdre's hands are crawling up and down inside her vest.

'What way are you going to do it?' I ask. Bowdre's the sort of man who has to wait until you ask him.

'Clubs, friend. A great chain of exotic key-clubs. Specially built to cater for the man who would like to lead an exotic life, but is still afraid of what his mother might say.

'I'm going to call my girls the Fishlettes,' he enthuses in his hoarse, dry voice. 'They'll wear plastic fishtails, and the entire club will be underwater. Bird's Eye cod steaks a speciality. The excitement of the deep without the dangers.'

Bowdre pours himself a full glass of brandy, and swallows half of it at once. His eyes are watering as he says: 'I can't lose. These girls will be the biggest draw since Mecca.

'The customers will be allowed to swim with them, dive with them, and dog-paddle with them. They won't be allowed to date them, and there'll be a rule against drowning in the same pool as the girls, but that won't put anybody off.

'Friend, this is the most erotic idea since the Titanic,' says Bowdre. 'We'll have all the best underwater entertainers in the world – Flipper, Lloyd Bridges, Jacques Cousteau, Hans and Lotte Hass.

'There's no danger of it getting out of hand,' Bowdre adds. 'Actually, there's nothing so quenching to the libido as swimming around in a soaking wet dinner jacket.'

A14 sits back in his chair in a wreath of smoke. He feels strangely drained and dull. He watches as the excited monkey-man strokes the girl's breasts and tickles her back. He says nothing at all.

'The clubs, of course, will be subject to Government approval,' puts in Samuel Baptist sitting down next to Bowdre and grinning at the girl.

(There is a dream – some kind of underwater birth – fish eyes stare glutinously from the dark – a cold touch of a green dying baby – the fishponds are alive with black wriggling spawn -)

A14 with dark memories of the agents of Tin Type Hall – just telling you Flipper won't be allowed to drown – the biggest idea since the Mecca dog-paddle – there's no danger of it getting out of water – I can't lose – the excitement of the erotic without the birth – all the best underwater hands –

'There's nothing so quenching to the entertainers as the legs of the girl's mother.'

'Is that you in black wriggling nest of hairs?'

'They won't be allowed to tickle the well-turned gong.'

All information on the Programme of Sliced Man – the Mysterious Babies breathe in the ear of Marcello Mastroianni – Lloyd Bridges, Mozart, Berlioz – they'll wear plastic vests – he sits back in a wreathe of breasts – the dying monkey-man grinning at the soaking wet thighs –

But it's too late. (As usual). The ice-cold breeze of Tin Type Hall is already misting up Charlie Bowdre's brandy glass. Frost is already forming on his moustache, and turning his hands to mottled blue and purple. He looks up, his cloudy eyes worried. His mouth has vanished with the draught.

The invisible door (there isn't one) swings open. Motherwell the Everlasting Erotica, his smile nailed to his face with ice, drifts into the room on silent castors.

(I stay in my chair, not moving. Perhaps if I don't move he won't notice me. I feel my cigarette is crackling loudly and giving me away. But I dare not crush it out.)

'Hallo, boys and girls,' says Motherwell in his age-old falsetto. 'It's such a lovely day outside – why don't you pull up the blinds?'

Baptist is standing up, but in agonising slow motion. His movements slur slowly across the sudden flash of light from the window, tying him in invisible cords. His mouth is pulling down to speak, but he can say nothing.

'Bowdre?' queries Motherwell, looking through

his file. 'Which one of you is Bowdre?'

The girl is somehow on the floor, in a strange tangle of dark limbs and breasts. Motherwell steps over her in one luminous stride and stands over Bowdre.

Bowdre's quaking. He's almost dissolved in a fog of white light that is glaring into the room. It eats his chair; it eats away his table and leaves him exposed to Motherwell (who is already leaning over him at an impossible angle, spangles of frost glittering in his hair).

'You're a silly boy, Charlie,' says Motherwell softly. 'If you had an underwater club, all the water would pour out into the street when you opened the door.'

Bowdre can say nothing. His nerveless fingers release the brandy glass, but it doesn't fall, Motherwell takes it gently and lays it somewhere in the dazzling light. Charlie's eyes have gone gray with fear.

A14 takes a flash photograph of the scene, and we have it here now, everything blotted out by light except for the worn back of Motherwell's coat and Bowdre's fingers clutching at the chair.

(I suddenly get this feeling this undressed girl on the carpet is the same girl I met at the hospital. She's older – her body has developed. She has different hair and a different face. But when she glances across at me with a frightened frown, I am sure it is her.)

BAPTIST: Motherwell!
MOTHERWELL: Don't do anything I wouldn't, Sammy.
BAPTIST: You won't –
(Sound of the girl whimpering. An indistinct scuffle

of feet on the floor. Something is knocked over – a glass, or a vase. One of the men grunts.)
MOTHERWELL: Now look what you've done!
BAPTIST: Crisp – help me stop him! Help me grab his arms!

(The recording is poor at this point. It appears that a coat or a cushion fell against the microphone. Motherwell is saying indistinctly: 'You've upset me now. You shouldn't have upset me.' There are more mutterings, followed by a prolonged battering sound.)

Motherwell fires his big black weapon from across the frightened room. His silencer is totally effective. We hear nothing but three high-pitched whistles as Bowdre (surprised) becomes plastered in red paint.

(Escape by old movies. There is a brief blur of old Western music and a scratching of a bad soundtrack as Motherwell makes good his escape.)

Charlie Bowdre is bleeding profusely. He is lying on his side with his face against the sofa, his right arm under him at an awkward angle. The girl is kneeling beside him, trying to stem the flow of blood with pages torn from his collection of erotic books.

'Best thing to do is call an ambulance,' says Baptist, now disinterested. He picks up one of the limp, bloodstained volumes and carries on reading where he left off.

I pick up the telephone, but it is dead. Motherwell probably destroyed the wires before he entered the building. Sweating, I run to the window and try to tear away the venetian blinds, but they're the sort that even karate experts can't damage. I set fire to the plastic slats with my cigarette lighter, and they flare up with a smell of burnt plastic.

The girl kept saying: 'Hurry, please' and her voice again reminds me of the child in the hospital. I can't make my arms co-ordinate properly, and the window appears to be jammed. Finally I smash the glass with my shoes. It tinkles into Grosvenor Square outside.

Leaning out into the early morning breeze, I see an elderly businessman in a bowler hat on the pavement below. He stares back up at me with a perplexed expression. I shout: 'Get an ambulance! For God's sake, hurry!'

The businessman pokes the broken glass on the paving stones around him with the tip of his umbrella. 'It's quite all right, thank you so much,' he calls back frigidly. 'I was protected from the worst of it by my bowler hat.'

'For the love of God!' I scream at him. 'There's a man dying up here! It's urgent!'

'Urgent or not, old boy,' replies the businessman crossly. 'There's no need to go throwing glass on a fellow.'

He turns and walks smartly off in the direction of Park Lane, only turning back once to scowl at me. I feel exhausted and panicky, and bite my lip.

Curiously, quietly, an ambulance arrives in the road outside. Two very tall ambulance men get out and walk into the building carrying a stretcher.

'They're here,' I tell Baptist softly. 'They've just arrived.'

'That was smart work,' he replies, turning a page.

But it is nearly ten minutes before the doorbell buzzes. The girl gets up from Bowdre's side and runs to answer it, the front of her vest and thighs smeared in blood. The two tall men stand efficiently in the hall.

They march in and lay their stretcher on the floor. They take a quick look around, then walk over to Bowdre, dying slowly on the carpet.

'You ought to be ashamed of yourself,' snaps one of the ambulance men, leaning over him and shaking his shoulder. 'Letting that young girl run around like that with a bullet wound. It's bloody amazing. You types spend half your time watching *Emergency Ward 10* on telly, and you don't even know how to keep a gunshot patient still and warm. Come on, Phil, let's get her to hospital.'

The ambulance men push the struggling girl on to the stretcher and hoist her up between them. She looks over at me desperately, but I can't think what to do. The ambulance men march quickly out of the door with her and begin to carry her downstairs.

Bowdre gives a bubbling groan. I suddenly get terribly frightened and run to the head of the stairs. I shout out: 'Hey!'

'Did you want something?' says the ambulance man testily. 'The girl – she's not the one you want. The man on the floor is dying up there.'

'Listen, mate,' replies the ambulance man. 'You do your job and I'll do mine, all right? If you don't know enough to keep a gunshot patient still and warm, how can you stand there and tell me what to do? So we'll just get on with it, and with a bit of luck we won't meet too many interfering people on the way to the hospital, and the girl might live.'

'You'd better go then,' I say dully. My mouth is sore and parched, and I sit on the head of the stairs, staring blankly at the wall.

After a few minutes, Baptist comes out carrying a book. 'I think he's dead,' he says. 'Would you mind coming in and having a look?'

So I spend a hard and miserable night on my concrete bunk in the red mesa corridor of Tin Type Hall. I awake with my eyes red and painful, and half-way through Shirley Temple in 'Rebecca of Sunnybrook Farm', which is flickering off the rough gray wall opposite my bed.

The old movies never stop. There is no soundtrack except for a confused blur of crackles and buzzing. Day after day, night after night, the worst films of the 1930's run interminably on the wall of my cell.

(You must remember there is no escape. I have forgotten what it means to escape there is no door on my cell; it is like a hermit's cave in a vast red concrete cliff. A fine choking dust blows across the flow, swirled into a pattern by the air conditioning. The thrum of turbines pulses through the dry, artificial air, at strange times of the night.)

Buzzzz – buzzzz – buzzzz – buzzzzzzz. (The film).

Scratching my neck, I sit up on the bunk and stare blankly at silver Shirley as she skips gaily in the dead sunlight of 1930. She pauses to stare back at me, then with cotton socks flying goes through the gate and fades out for ever.

'You're a fool, Shirley,' I whisper under my breath. Then get up unsteadily and go to the door of my cell to look out into the unending Greek-key corridors of Tin Type Hall.

I have lost all sense of time. I do not even know whether I am sleeping at night or day. My cell is lit with a bland, fluorescent light from an unseen source. It makes me insufferably fatigued, and I can no longer think logically. I am developing nervous delusions, and have a persistent image of a black cat, creeping just out of line with my vision. When I turn to face it, it is gone. Once I went down on my hands and knees to comb the dusty floor for hairs.

The film has now changed to a 1920 version of 'Rasputin'. I have a trick of being able to look at the movies quite objectively, so that the picture is no longer coherent, but merely a shifting pattern on the wall. It helps to relieve the boredom.

I have had visitors, but I cannot remember who they were. I have an impression that there was a fat man, but I cannot be sure. I recall the visits now only as snatches of isolated, magnetic conversation. I may have imagined them. It is hard to tell.

(Back on the beach the sun is so hot that it blisters my eyelids. I climb to my feet in the suffocating heat and walk slowly through the spiky, equatorial grass. I rest against the dry, gray trunk of a coconut palm; my feet surrounded by hairy husks, and light a cigarette. He smiles.)

Suddenly I am talking to a large man in a creaking basketwork chair. There is a small glass-topped table beside him (visual joke of 'Alice in Wonderland') with a bottle of sweet sherry on it. The man takes a glass in his pudgy hand and fills it.

'You are beginning to grow tired,' he says. It is not a question, but a statement of fact. He knows I am tired. He has seen many tired people before.

'One finds that one does grow tired after an extended time in the Hall. It is a (necessary) part of the stay. We try hard to entertain our visitors, but we have several, and it is not always easy to give them our undivided attention.'

I sit on my bunk with my chin in my hands and stare at the man. He is wearing a white tropical dinner-jacket, with pink stains of sweat under the armpits. He is almost bald, with a few stray hairs floating from his scalp like fuse-wire. He has an alarming cast in his black-dotted eyes, and they seem to swivel independently to glance round the cell.

The cell itself has become like the Beachcomber Bar at Butlins of Bognor Regis. There are artificial palm trees, and a crude mural of a South Sea beach, dotted with boats and coconuts. Flickering Hawaiian music drones in the background.

'Entertainment is so much a part of life,' says the fat man dully. 'All work and no play makes George a dull boy.'

'Jack, I always say.' It is the first time I have spoken for months, and the word is harsh. I realise I have a sore throat.

'What?' says the man, rotating one or his eyes towards me.

'Jack,' I repeat. 'It's not "All work and no play makes George a dull boy" – it's "All work and no play makes Jack a dull boy".'

'Is it?' replies the fat man, expressionlessly. 'Well I always say George.'

'You're entitled to say what you like,' I tell him. 'But the correct version is Jack.'

'I didn't know that,' the fat man says sourly, taking a large swallow of sherry. 'But then, nobody's been rude enough to point it out to me before.'

'I'm not being rude. I'm just trying to tell you what the correct version is, so that you don't say the wrong thing next time you're in company.'

'I couldn't care less about company,' the fat man tells me in a biting voice. 'I say George and I will continue to say George. If you don't like it, you know what you can do about it.'

I'm feeling tired, and there's a sickening pit of hunger in my stomach. I lean forward weakly over my knees and draw patterns in the dust with my finger. I can't make this man out. I don't even want to try. He's invaded my privacy, and he's a bore. I make it clear that I don't really want to speak to him at all.

'I haven't come to see you as a favour,' the fat man begins, more sternly than before, but not angry any more. 'I'm not a welfare officer or a Red Coat. My name is Hilary Starfessed, and I am the Executive Manager of Tin Type Hall.'

'Shall I applaud?'

'You can if you like. It all depends, sir, on whether you want to jeopardise the outcome of your case. I am a patient man, Mr Crisp, but I will not tolerate facetiousness. I take things slowly and carefully, and there is no room in my tasks for flippant comments. You understand me?'

'I understand, I suppose.'

'Splendid. A little understanding goes a long way. Every cloud has a silver ending. Now let's get down to business.'

Hilary Starfessed, fat executive manager of Tin Type Hall, eyes me carefully and sips at his sweet amber sherry. He suffers from adenoids, and his breathing is hard and whining.

'You must appreciate (Mr Crisp) why I am here. I am here to see that you have a (fair deal, reasonable treatment, a good chance). We are in an invidious position as far as you are concerned, a bird in the bush being as good as an empty pitcher.

'Our alternatives are to hand you over to the police and indict you for trespass, or to hold to summary inquiry to investigate your intentions toward Tin Type Hall.'

I tell him softly: 'I have no intentions, as you put it, to Tin Type Hall. I am here, I am shut up. I have no intentions.'

'Not even to be free?' says Hilary casually, pouring himself another full glass of sherry.

(I don't know. It's impossible for me to say. I have lost all contact with 'free'. I am not imprisoned, but I cannot leave. I don't want to answer that question. Why did you have to ask it? Why don't you leave me alone?)

'I am trying to do my best for you, Mr Crisp. Please appreciate that I am using all means (at my disposal) to do what I can for you. I am a busy man, and I am using all means. Don't try to evade my questions. Still waters run in time.'

Marlene Dietrich in old film cuts out Hilary Starfessed and blurs into flickering images of 1946. Someone (a holy man) is making a long and detailed speech, but it is impossible to hear exactly what he is saying. I put my fingers in my ears, but the buzzing vibrates through my jawbone.

(The girl is laughing at something. There is a fat man in white at her elbow. He is explaining some legal point at great length, and drinking at great speed. She turns to him, and unexpectedly draws down the front of her evening dress, exposing her pink nipples.)

'A summary inquiry of course,' he is saying, 'will put you more into the care of Tin Type Hall than into strict legal provinces. It is up to you to decide which you prefer.'

'I prefer neither. I just want to be left alone. Please go and leave me alone. I have a headache.'

Hilary Starfessed shakes his head. The shaking remains in the air, indelibly marked in soft herringbone waves.

The sugary smell of the sherry makes my stomach lurch.

'Impossible, I'm afraid. There is an enormous amount of paper-work involved here. A great many people have spent a great amount of (time and effort) trying to sort out your case, and give you the fairest deal possible. You must co-operate.'

'Would Jack Beauregard have co-operated?'

'I don't know what you mean. Please try to stick to the point. I have never heard of anyone of that name. I am a civil servant. I am responsible for the welfare of the people in this district, and I must obey orders. I am trying to do for you what I can. I am stretching the rules quite considerably.'

And so the interview continues, possibly for another three or four hours. The sherry glass is filled repeatedly, and the basketwork chair creaks and squeaks with Hilary Starfessed's patient movements. I am so tired that my eyes have gone out.

All over the city, art nouveau is taking over the wires. Electric buzzing blocks the telephone lines and the lights are flickering a dull green. Through the darkening streets, Motherwell the Everlasting Executioner paces the city, his lethal weapon in hand. The doors shiver. The streets shiver. Just telling you hi-ho etc.

Three days before the killing of Jack Beauregard, a Knightsbridge perambulator shop has a visit from an unusual party of women. The details of the incident are not clearly known, but it is understood that there were several eye-witnesses, including Workman Bill and the Famous Ear.

The manager of the Baby Bubbles Infant Carriage shop is 42-year old Mr Cecil Brolac, a slender man who wears pink shirts and green mohair suits. His chin has a turquoise shadow, and his cheeks are laced with veins.

'I was standing just here,' he says, pointing to the folding cot display. 'My assistant, Miss Vel, had gone to Woolworths next door to get me a cup of tea and a salmon sandwich.'

The pixie bell above the shop door is brought to an abrupt silence by the muscular hand of a six-foot matron in heavy tweeds and wellington boots.

She marches to the centre of the shop, followed by a bevy of six pretty young girls, all blonde, with short skirts and wide made up eyes.

'Shop!' she shouts, casting her leathery face from side to side, like a worn football being punted over a field of tweed.

Cecil Brolac comes forward nervously, rubbing his hands. For some reason, he gives a polite little bow. The booted matron stares at him, grimly. Behind her, the nymphets stand bemused.

'Perhaps I could point out madarm, that this is not a shop, but a boutique,' explains Cecil. His haughty tone is not very confident.

'I don't care if you're a coal yard, *man*,' grates the matron, pulling him aside. She spits out the word 'man' as if it were the greatest insult she can muster. To Cecil, actually, it is rather a compliment.

'Did madarm want a pram, or baby goods of any sorts?' asked Cecil, fluttering about the shop with a mauve feather duster.

Again, the six-foot woman shoves him out of her way. 'Something of the sort, something of the sort,' she mutters.

Cecil hovers around her wincing as she tests every pram by bouncing them violently up and down on their springs. She kicks the wheels with her giant boots, and wrests the hoods up and down with her powerful hands.

'If madarm could give me some idea of what she wants –' suggests Cecil, dodging between the matron and a range of expensive pushchairs.

(In 1910, my grandfather saw a thin, ragged boy in the streets. He walked over to him, touched by the boy's condition, and offered him a half-crown. The boy looked up at him and snarled: 'Garn, shitface.')

But by now the matron and her cortège of sexy blondes have reached the end of their battering tour of the Baby Bubbles Infant Carriage shop. They stand in an uncompromising line, the leathery woman in the centre, like a firing squad.

'Something small, madarm, or possibly something a little larger?' suggests Cecil Brolac limply. His left eye is fluttering semaphore signals to the street.

'We have the Biddy-Boo Walker or the Diddumskar, or the Humpty-Pram,' continues Cecil. 'I can show you the latest line in Bar-Bar-Cots.'

The matron grimaces, '*Man,*' and turns her back on him. She whispers loudly to her girls for nearly five minutes, and then advances on Cecil again.

'We want something large,' she snaps. 'Something that's built to last. Something of toughened steel, with solid wheels, and hefty axles, can you oblige, *man*?'

Cecil bites his lip. He is not looking well, as you

may have noticed. He sits down behind the counter and draws aimless patterns on his receipt book.

After a few seconds, though, his eye cocks up brightly. He raises his hand confidingly to the matron, and walks out through the curtain at the back of the shop.

The matron waits impatiently. Then there is the squeaking of heavy wheels from outside, and Cecil Brolac, bright scarlet in the face, comes into the shop wheeling a British Railways platform trolley. He hauls it to a halt, and leans against it proudly, perspiring.

'This was left outside after the last stock delivery, madarm,' he pants. 'You are most welcome to it if it meets your needs.'

The matron's face suddenly cracks into a smile, and she fondles Cecil's chin with a raspy hand. She throws a pillow and blankets on to the trolley, and takes a pound note out of a tight crocodile-skin purse to pay for them.

The girls, their blonde hair waving, clamber aboard the trolley and lie down in a giggling heap. The matron seizes the handles and pushes them majestically out of the Baby Bubbles Shop.

Cecil opens the door for them, and smiles as they steam pass. He notices before he shuts up shop that the streets are strangely dark for this time of night, and there is a chilly wind blowing.

Had a visitor to my silver cell once. I whisper under my breath 'the Greek-key version of 1910'. I have a trick of shifting strange films of the night. A black cat is lit with pulses of no escape. He kept eyeing me …

Dead sunlight of Cold Sun. Just remember the mind's drop in sometime. It makes me insufferably dull, and there is no room for a long and detailed jawbone. The Programme of Sliced Man whistles Mysterious Babies in locked suitcase. Just telling you hi-ho.

'Perfume your undies by putting empty bottles in your drawers.'

'Government may ease Bill's passage.'

It's taking me back, the Mysterious Babies case. The music of Johnson Willow, sad vendor of Charlotte Street, drifts across the darkening wires of London. His eyes peer out from behind the dead varnished bellies of his mandolin.

'I am going to write a symphony in varying shades of silence.'

'Is that you …?'

The story, the story of Jack Beauregard. Try to remember as the night falls and starlings perch on the electric cables of the city. Electric buzzing crackles in the sky, and the cleaners are silent and taciturn as they go about their evening work.

We next see him walking towards Somerset House, just as dark is settling. He is dressed in the long fawn raincoat that is to become famous in years to come. His eyes are gray and steady, and there is no hint of the shots on the pavements of Haymarket.

BEAUREGARD: I wish to register a death.
CLERK: Certainly, sir. What is the name?
BEAUREGARD: James Beauregard.
CLERK: Occupation?
BEAUREGARD: Eater of Cities.
CLERK: Date of the death, sir?
BEAUREGARD: In about four years' time.

He is at this time involved in a brutal deal for Tin Type

Hall. He has been ordered to search out and eliminate a new housing estate in Shepperton. 'The residents are soulless, even though we have done all we can for them,' says Hilary Starfessed, executive manager.

Jack arrives at the estate one afternoon in his brown Standard van. He draws up outside one of the plain, modern brick houses and gets out. He walks carefully up the path and knocks on the door.

A grubby little boy in a red jumper with a piece of bread and jam in his hand opens the door. Jack Beauregard smiles at him absently and says: 'Is your mummy in?'

The mother comes to the door in a flowered apron and curlers. She screws up her eyes against the Cadet cigarette in her lips.

'My name is Beauregard, madam,' says Jack quietly. 'I've come about your daughter.'

'Jennie, you mean,' replies the woman suspiciously. 'What about 'er?'

'I've made her pregnant.' smiles Jack.

The woman looks at him for a few moments. Then she says: 'Well, you better come in, then.'

Jack Beauregard steps into the hall, cluttered with old copies of the Daily Mirror and smelling of children's urine. His feet crunch on bits of broken toys. (Over the rooftops, a red white and blue kite.)

'This is Mr Bogard, dad,' says the woman loudly. ''E says 'e's put Jennie in the family way.'

The father looks Jack up and down, and scratches his ear. He makes no attempt to turn down the television, and doesn't move from his chair.

''Ave yer?' he says. 'What you do that for, then?'

'If I could sit down, perhaps I could explain,' Jack says in a pained voice. The wife takes a heap of comics and newspapers off the blue plastic upholstered sofa, and throws them on the floor. Jack sits down tentatively, and says: 'Thank you.'

(We have a very special audience here tonight, folks, from the Sunnyrest Home for the Criminally Insane. Each one of the contestants has a chance to go on the treasure Trail, and win themselves £20,000 worth of Chinese manure. Here's our perky Cockney assistant, Monica Dwarf, and Emlyn Glynne-Davis, that magnificent Welsh tenor, will sing requests.)

Beauregard is saying: 'I did not want to take advantage of your daughter. But the truth is we love each other. One thing just followed another.'

The father, without taking his eyes off the TV, replies: "Ow much d'you earn? I mean, when she 'as it, can yer afford to support 'er – give 'er the good 'ome she's used ter? She's been very well brought up, yer know. I always said 'er mother spoils 'er, but yer know what mothers are.'

'Yes, I know what mothers are.'

(So you want to answer questions on Female Homosexuality! I see. How about that, folks, this very venerable old Chelsea pensioner wants to answer questions on female homosexuality! That's a very unusual hobby, sir, if I may say so, for a man your age. I understand you fought in the Somme in the Great War, sir? Oh, you were in Berlin. But they're not far away from each other, are they? And did you win any medals? I mean, apart from the Iron Cross?)

'I am an educated man,' states Beauregard loudly. 'I have a degree in ichthyology.'

'Oh yes,' says the father. 'What's that when it's at home?'

'The study of fish. I'm a Catholic, you see, and the

exam was on a Friday. I really wanted to take zoology, but I had no choice.'

The mother says helpfully: 'You could 'ave confessed it, couldn't you?'; through her waggling Cadet.

(For a pound, sir – if you don't mind standing a bit closer – yes, I know I've got bad breath, but they have to get us both in – for a pound: Was Lesbian any relation to Brendan Behan?)

'Would you like a cup of tea?' says the mother. Beauregard smiles, but says no. he is not a tea drinker. Chimpanzees drink tea on television, and that put him off it for good.

'I'd just like to explain,' he comments, almost shouting above 'Double Your Money', 'that I am prepared to take full responsibility for your daughter's condition, and make an honest woman of her by taking her to the altar. I certainly wouldn't like to see her subjected to gossip and persecution, and neither would I like any child of mine to be called a bastard.'

The father suddenly looks round at Beauregard roughly. He is gripping his glass of warm pale ale in his hand, and there is a ring of foam round his lips.

'Look, mate,' he says. 'I've never met you before, and without being personal you're not the sort of bloke I'd give up me dinner hour to get to know. I don't mind yer barging in 'ere and carrying on about fish and our Jennie and one flaming thing following another, but I do expect yer to keep a bloody civil tongue in yer 'ead. If you want to call me a bastard, we'll keep it straight and go outside and settle it man to man, as soon I've watched me programme.'

'But I wasn't –' begins Beauregard.

'Dad 'e didn't call you what you said,' interrupts

the mother condescendingly. 'You always get 'old of the wrong end of the flippin' stick, you do. I don't know (to Jack), I called him impetuous once and 'e thought I meant his flies was undone. No flippin' education, that's 'is trouble.'

The father has almost forgotten his programme. He shouts: 'Look, woman, when I was a youngster I 'ad to go out and earn a bloody crust just to keep me family alive. I did a fourteen-hour day in a bloody baked bean factory, and I wasn't arguing. You couldn't bloody argue if yer mum and yer brothers and sisters was dependin' on yer. There wasn't no bloody time for no bloody degrees in no bloody fish, and if yer want to argue about who's the better man, I'm quite bloody prepared to go outside and settle it man-to-man. Now, let's just watch this programme, shall we?'

(You are in a sealed soundproof box, sir, for your £8,000 Treasure Trail question on female homosexuality. Can you hear me? I said, can you hear me? Sir, are you able to hear what I'm saying? (Pause) Monica, will you please run and fetch an Ever-Ready 15-volt – his deaf aid battery's faded out. Won't be a moment now, folks, before the £8,000 question on female homosexuality!)

The living-room door opens, and an untidy-looking schoolgirl with a white face and wrinkled stockings slouches in. At the sight of her, the mother's mouth goes into a hard line, and she cuffs the girl on to the sofa next to Beauregard.

'Right, young madam,' she snaps. 'Now you're going to tell me all about it.'

'About what, mum?' drones the girl. From the corner of his eye, Jack can see that she is singularly unattractive. Making love to her would be like having an affair with a female Harpo Marx. He winces in his grandmotherly way, but says nothing.

'About you and Mr Bogard 'ere. You and your goings-on behind my back. Yu slut!'

'I never saw 'im before in my life!' protests the girl. ''Oo is 'e, anyway?'

'Don't you lie to me –' rages the mother, but Jack is already on his feet and laying a cultured and restraining hand on her arm. He bows slightly.

'I'm afraid your daughter is quite right,' he tells her warmly. 'There's been a little mistake. It appears I have come to the wrong house.'

'Oh,' says the mother. She is obviously quite disappointed at having nothing further to be furious about. She begins to fuss this way and that, making unnecessary adjustments to the chair seat covers and the plaster ornaments.

'Well, I better see you out then,' she says at last, rubbing her hands. Beauregard says: 'Quite so.'

The father looks up long enough to grunt: 'Cheerio, mate.' And then Jack is back in the bald street of the housing estate, smiling quietly to himself and preparing to carry out his instructions.

(No, I'm so sorry, sir, 'yogurt' is not an acceptable answer. Give a sincere hand, please, for this surprisingly old pensioner. I'm terribly sorry, sir. But the best of luck in the future, what you have of it. Next contestant, please!)

3

a man of conscience

So she stops singing. And the gray shabby London flat is nervous suddenly with her no-singing and the reed-like patterns of early evening are criss-crossing the curtains and the chairs.

'There's no need to stop,' says Jack Beauregard in a soft voice. 'I was quite enjoying it.'

He is eating a fried goldfish sandwich and smoking a cigarette. There is chalk on his lapels which may have rubbed off a wall.

Earlier, there is a call from Rufus Shack, who is watching the Venables Street entrance of Tin Type Hall. He sounds tired and worried, and the noise of his fingers scratching his beard is amplified over the phone.

('Some sort of convention – possibly the Mysterious Babies may be there – I've been watching them coming and going for two hours now – hard to tell what to do – just telling you to drop in sometime.')

Rufus is a short bulgy-eyed man with a harsh, mocking sense of humour. He is fond of trad jazz and beer, and his face is mottled with ginger freckles. Another of his gimmicks is old Chinese insults.

'Suitable greeting, oh employer of my humble services,' he grins at me two days before the assignation of Jack Beauregard.

'Good morning Rufus,' I reply, not looking up from the morning editions spread on my desk.

'No! No! No!' he howls, slapping his thigh. 'You're supposed to answer: "May the Unseeing guide your footsteps … into a vat of boiling sulphur!"'

I stare at him with eyes slitted, but he is still very much in evidence. He watches me with half-surprised expression as I put a call through to Father Boniface, our aging soft-eyed chief reporter.

(FLASHBACK TO HAYMARKET: As Jack Beauregard the Eater of Cities fly dives like a paper plane. The streets revolve around him in rapid, scuttling steps. There is a high-pitched singing noise in his ears, and the distant sound of voices and traffic. Someone is saying: 'May be dead …')

Charlie Bowdre, found dead and blue-lipped on the floor of his Grosvenor Square flat, is to be buried today at St Augustine's Church, South Croydon, where he was confirmed by the Bishop of Southwark in 1928. As Reporter A14 puts on his raincoat, he notices that the sky is already a metallic gray, and there is a humid odour of electricity in the air.

The church is a square building of dark flint. It is crowded next to a hideous red-brick church hall, and is decorated with stucco like second-hand custard. It is overgrown with long tangled grass and weeds. The houses in the area are crumbling suburban maisonettes, fenced with broken wooden slats or shrivelled brown hedges.

The funeral service is over when A14 arrives in his black Morris Minor. He parks it behind a fleet of glossy hire cars and locks it. Funeral guests are notorious thieves.

('He was dead, so he didn't have any use for it,' explains a worn-looking man in Paddington magistrate's court. He is obviously poor – his black tie is a raincoat belt, and his black armband has Borough of Marylebone' stitched on it in red letters. He sniffles from time to time into a crumpled piece of Kleenex.

'Is the owner going to testify?' asks the chairman, an elderly woman in a green hat and thick-lensed spectacles.

'Yes, madam,' speaks up a faceless solicitor. 'They're just combing the crematorium gardens for him now.')

The coffin, with Charlie Bowdre in it, is shouldered carefully out of the church and into the scrubby churchyard. The guests are already standing round the open grave, and white handkerchiefs are fluttering in the sticky breeze. Reporter A14 walks quietly up and joins them, sniffling slightly because of his hay fever.

There are some interesting faces among the mourners. At the head of the grave, admiring the polished marble tombstone is Gordon Casper, one-time friend of Jack Beauregard. He is pale-faced, and wearing a badly fitting blue suit. Reporter A14 notices that Casper is wearing odd shoes.

Amidst the little knot of friends and relatives stands Monsieur Retaud, immaculately black-suited, and carrying a black cane. Leaning on his arm is Gaylord Smith, whom A14 recognises as a blonde stripper from Dean Street. Retaud's previous mistress,

Janine Blown, has obviously met with disfavour. He hears later that he put a drop of cyanide in her Ovaltine.

Hilary Starfessed, executive manager of Tin Type Hall, is not present. But two of his hired men (Mozart, Berlioz) are standing silently in the long churchyard grass watching the proceedings from a respectful distance.

There is only one man that A14 does not know. He is talking quietly to one of Bowdre's younger relatives, a woman of 84 who is shrivelled but extremely rich. The man is handsome in a cold way, with wavy blond hair and a long pale jaw. He is dressed in a tailored gray suit, and has a black tulip in his lapel. He is saying something about: '... the yacht, of course, was rather shallow in draught ... obviously, at this time of year ... drop in sometime ...'

But now there is the sound of shouting from the church entrance, as the vicar is accompanied out by two sour-faced sidesmen.

The vicar has been amputated from the groin downwards, after an accident at a diocesan meeting which has never been clearly explained. He transports himself on a metal frame, rather like an electric tea-trolley, with small castors at the bottom.

The trolley is very complicated to manoeuvre, and the vicar is having difficulty driving out of the church. It seems that the clutch is jammed, and he is going round and round in circles at great speed in the vestibule.

'Get away, damn you!' he bellows at the sidesmen as they come to his assistance. 'If I can't make the damn thing work by now, I never will!'

Finally, red-faced and wheezing, he pulls himself

to a halt. Then, slowly and carefully, he guides the trolley out on to the gravelled path of the churchyard and approaches the grave.

'My apologies for the delay,' he says fiercely. 'My wife insists on parking me in the vicarage garage, and my battery's flat.'

Humming softly, the electric vicar circles the little bunch of mourners and pulls himself up with a squeak of brakes beside the coffin.

Reporter A14 takes a quick look round the guests to detect any emotion. But they are all silent and expressionless, and the young man in the gray suit is looking out over the road at an old woman cutting her hedge.

'Earth, which God hath created, receive thy son Charles Edwin Bowdre, and be truly thankful,' grumbles the vicar. The moist warm wind stirs the weeds and grasses, and the little gathering is perspiring in silence.

'Ashes to ashes, dust to dust, and may God have mercy on his soul, amen,' the vicar says.

There is a pause, rather long and uncomfortable. The vicar doesn't appear to have anything more to say, and is resting his chin on his hand. His trolley is buzzing and humming again like a train waiting at a station.

After five minutes, the reverie breaks suddenly. He turns to the sidesmen and shouts: 'What the hell are you waiting for? Chuck him in!'

(The Captain of Kodak peers out from behind the graveyard wall, takes a flash photograph of the burial and disappears. It is growing late, and the picture when it is developed is peculiarly dim. The Captain shrugs and lights a cigarette.)

Walking back to their cars, A14 approaches the man in the gray suit. The man doesn't appear surprised to see him, but obviously doesn't know who he is.

'Did you know Charlie Bowdre well?' asks A14 politely.

'Not at all, in fact, I'm afraid,' replies the man apologetically.

'Would it be rude to ask why you're here, then?' says A14.

'Of course not. I'm interested in a fellow called John Remorse, also known as the Serjeant of Time Film. A friend of mine called me and said he might be here. I came along to see if I could trace him. It doesn't look as though I've had much luck, though.'

A14 nods. 'You might be luckier than you think. I know of John Remorse. In fact, I have a particular interest in him, like you. Listen, here is my office phone number. Ring me up and we'll have a talk about him.'

The conversation is short. A14 can gather from it only that the young man is well educated, and possibly of Irish ancestry. The man's name is Paul Szondi.

There has been a thunderstorm, but it hasn't relieved the oppressive heat. The streets are measled with warm spots of rain, and the clouds are a dark green, like tarnished copper. There has been no news of the Mysterious Babies. I am tired, and the electricity of the day is fading.

I am sitting in the kitchen of Bridget Segrave's Kensington flat, perched on a table, drinking cocoa and smoking. Bridget is telling me about her father.

'My father was the only real Man of Conscience

that I've ever known. When all his business associates fell by the wayside, you know, getting involved in off-colour deals, he absolutely abstained from doing anything that might implicate him.'

I nod but say nothing. I'm expecting a call from the night editor, George Macfries, at any moment, and I'm only half-listening.

'I suppose he didn't make as much money as he could have done, because of his conscience,' says Bridget. 'But it must be marvellous to reach the end of one's life and still be a whole man.'

Yes, yes, I nod. Although it worries me, because I don't feel whole, I feel instead shattered into millions of fragments, grating against each other inside my skin like broken mirror stuck to transparent tape. Each mirror reflects Mandrake the Magician as he peers round the corners of London. Each mirror reflects the microcosm of our lighted kitchen, set in the glistening flesh of the city, and the watchmaker with his hands of clockwork cogs is sitting in the Wimpy Bars of the West End.

It could be the same girl. There is a marked resemblance. I look at Bridget Segrave, at the thin dark nape of her neck, at the way she holds her cigarette poised in that particular crooked position, and it has to be her. The girl at the hospital, the girl in Charlie Bowdre's flat. Just telling you it has to be her.

'Are you listening?' she says. The unnatural light in the kitchen makes this seem like a film. From time to time the blue gas in the Ascot flares to heat the water. Someone is leaning out of a window somewhere and singing 'Lilli Bolero'.

'I'd like to write a book about him, you know, Tom,' she says. 'I'd call it *A Man of Conscience*. The first part would be a portrait of him as his wife sees him – my mother. The second part would show you what his business associates think of him, and the third part would be from his children's point of view. In that way you could build up a three-dimensional impression of him, and draw your own conclusions.'

'You're very close to him, aren't you?' I remark. 'I've never known what it's like to be as close to a parent as that.'

To write a book about him. To tell the story of a man who is my father, and his completely different life, and the days he's spent and the thoughts he's had that I know nothing about. And what about my grandfather, who I last saw sitting in dim gray light of a Sunday afternoon, pale and drawn and close to death, discussing with me in his dry, tired voice the medals he'd won for science in Paris in 1910, but 1910 never came alive for me, and three months afterwards he was cremated.

(But you remember Henry West. He was the unfortunate young man who was swept off the roof of the Great Western Railway Station in Reading on March 24, 1840, and killed. The inscription on his grave reads:

Sudden the change, I in a moment fell,
And had not time to bid my friends farewell.
Yet hushed be all complaint – 'tis sweet, 'tis blessed
To change Earth's stormy scenes for endless rest.
Dear friends, prepare, take warning by my fall,
So you shall hear with joy your Saviour's call.)

Was Henry West a man of principle? Or was he too young, and smashed into glass? Remember the mind's representative. Remember Motherwell the Everlasting Executioner pacing the streets of the city with his cold and lethal weapon in hand.

Yes, yes, I am nodding like a whole man. Set in the wheelie Railway pale and drawn with a marked resemblance. But you remember each other inside my skin. He absolutely abstained from the think dark nape of gas. It gives me flares and smashed to stormy scenes of science. Paris in 1910, and so you shall hear with joy. Just telling you he was the unfortunate man of conscience.

I suppose he didn't make the inscription. In that way, you could build up a three-dimensional programme of 'Sliced Man'. How much does it cost to say he kept eyeing me. To write a grandfather of the Medal of Microcosm. But you remember Henry Saviour.

Johnson Willow the sad music vendor of Charlotte Street has miniature tape-recorders set in his front teeth. When he opens his mouth to smile, you can see the tiny transparent wheels revolving. He uses the recorders to pick up shreds of music from the streets, then plays them back in his mouth when he's in bed. He turns his soft spaniel eyes to me and says coyly: 'You'll never guess where the batteries are ...'

I am talking to Johnson over half-pints of bitter in a miserable Brickwood's pub somewhere near Victory Street. There is a stack of unhealthy-looking meat rolls under a plastic cover, and the air is thick with Old Holborn smoke.

(It turns out – he is a one-time drinking partner of Paul Szondi – the man I am to meet four days later at Charlie Bowdre's funeral. He explains to me as much as he knows of Szondi – in between his musical words taking mean sips at his beer -)

Paul Szondi is a psychiatrist. Before he took his doctorate at Heidelberg in 1958, he was a world champion rock scrambler. A very energetic sport, requiring great poise and equally great stamina. Szondi was a perfectionist, and would cycle around Alpine villages with a dead cow trailing behind his bicycle to get into training.

He was married at the age of 24 to Marsha van Doepnts, who was 30 years older than he, considerably richer, and had at one time been the favourite pupil of Isadora Duncan.

Marsha had adored Isadora. She would take Paul's lean muscular hand in her own white withered palms and say wistfully: 'I gave her presents you know, Paul. On special occasions, I gave her scarves. Dear Isadora always choked up when I gave her a scarf ...'

She loved Paul because he was 'such a young, vibrant, butterfly of a creature.' She brought him expensive gifts (he still has the gold watch she gave him), and fed him on exotic foods. He took the gifts, but refused to eat lark's tongues, because he was in training.

Secretly, Paul loathed his middle-aged wife. The marriage had seemed an excellent union to begin with, and he had boasted of his 'deeper appreciation of middle-aged women'. But after six months of living together, he began to feel that her nauseating body and her revolting personal habits far outweighed the status of being married to a 'personality'.

'Why do you have to bleed?' he screamed at her in the Grand Hotel in Koln, one miserable autumn night in 1956. But she would only smother him with affection and kisses, and he felt disgusted at her touch, as though she was a reptile.

One day he climbed to a wild cleft in the Dolomites called Maschetz Cranny. On his own in the rank grass, almost overpowered by stinking weeds, he broke open a bottle of Chianti and rechristened the gorge 'Marsha's Fanny'.

'It smells the same, it sounds the same, it's just as deep and twice as rough,' he chanted. 'The only way you can tell the difference is that Marsha hasn't got a village in her left thigh.'

(Marsha died – pistol shots – Vienna. Paul expected vast legacy – was told March 23 1957 a dark day in Basle – 'She left it all to the Stray Dugong Fund in Mauritius' – so broke and depressed, waited impatiently in Zurich for 'something to turn up', like a man trying to concentrate while dying to go to the loo –)

The wires are humming today. Tin Type Hall, its messages floating like purple ash across the uncertain sky. The convention of the Mysterious Babies. The unknown destination of John Remorse, Serjeant of Time Film. Are you ready for what is to come?

'You must realise – may be dead.'

'Why do you have to eye me.'

'Is that you? Could almost feel Cold Sun ...'

Evening falls and the sky is charged with dense electricity. There is a smell of smouldering copper in the air. I walk through Kensington with pale face and nervous hands. Do you remember the mind's agent. It is impossible now to distinguish what is going on. Everything is so blurred. Everything is so fogged with light. There appears to be some movement – an arm, a wrist – but it's impossible to say.

There is a buzz at the door. Someone is standing outside in the corridor, pressing their flat white nose against the glass. Bridget puts down her coffee and goes to answer it. I lean back against the wall to see who it is.

'Dry rot men,' announces the Famous Ear, stepping uninvited into the hall. He is followed closely by Workman Bill, who is puffing at a diminutive black cigarette.

'What for?' Bridget says sharply. 'I never knew you were coming. What have you got to do?'

'The dry rot,' says the Famous Ear, looking around the hall with appreciative eyes. Workman Bill nods his head towards the door and adds: 'We've come up to do your dry rot.'

'Well, I don't think we have seen any dry rot,' Bridget tells them, rather forlornly.

The Famous Ear digs the heel of his concrete-encrusted boot into the carpet. 'Wanna bet?' he says.

'If you think there is, you'd better start in there,' Bridget tells them, and opens the door of the living room. 'And you can tell the landlord that I'm annoyed about this. Be careful with the ornaments.' She comes back into the kitchen frowning slightly.

Workman Bill falls immediately into one of the arm chairs and takes out his Old Holborn tin. He pinches a few shreds of tobacco and pushes them with a clumsy finger along a piece of liquorice paper. He rolls the cigarette up, and gives it a large wet lick.

'Where we going ter start then, Famous?' he asks.

He touches the end of his cigarette with his old petrol lighter, and it flares up in his lips and vanishes. He is left with nothing in his mouth but a bit of black ash.

The Famous Ear, arms akimbo, looks about. Then he says: 'A stick of the yeller in the chandelier oughta do it.'

Workman Bill fumbles in his canvas sack and produces a single stick of dynamite. The Famous Ear meanwhile is dragging a chair across under the chandelier and climbing up on to it. Balanced precariously, he takes out a fuse and matches, and asks Bill to hand him up the charge.

'You ready then?' he shouts, and drops the lighted dynamite into the light bowl. Together, the Famous Ear and Workman Bill dive for cover behind the chaise-lounge.

There is a deafening blast, and the room is filled with thick brown smoke. As it rises slowly, it reveals shattered floorboards, burnt skeletal chairs, and long strips of plaster hanging from the ceiling.

The Famous Ear emerges from the room with thick clunk of splintered wood in his hand. He holds it up so that Bridget and I can see it.

'Lost me bet,' he says. 'You're all right fer dry rot.'

(And, again, it is summer. We are sitting at a table overlooking the sea, which is still and warm. A rock-and-roll band is playing in the darkness – Beatles with an unfamiliar Chinese accent. The loudspeaker is lodged in a palm tree, and it is so hot that even iced Tiger beer doesn't help.)

They are after us now. We know that. The Programme of Sliced Man is to go into operation any day. Motherwell the Everlasting Executioner has not been seen for weeks, and it is suspected that he has flown to Buenos Aires with Hilary Starfessed. Our laboratories are inspecting the bank-note fragments, but so far they have come up with nothing. We do not know at this time that Jack Beauregard is a marked man. But we are aware that Tin Type Hall is moving quietly into operation.

(It's raining. Do you remember, Barbara …)

The rain did compel a
Young lady named Ella
To wait in a cellar.

A fella said tell 'er
I'll sell 'er
A yella umbrella.

(The story so far. Dashing, daredevil Paul Szondi, also known as Envoy John, alias Starving Eamonn Midnight, is on his way to Tin Type Hall, office of the evil plotters, to trace his long-lost cousin, John Remorse, who was last seen smiling up the White Nile in a hired xebec. Paul has been seeing a lot lately of Janine Blown, former mistress of the mysterious Monsieur Retaud, and it is suspected that he is trying to blackmail her previous lover. Little does he know that Gordon Casper, and old friend of Retaud, is racing to Worthing Central Station to try and find William Turner, an associate of Reporter A14, in an attempt to discover the whereabouts of the Mysterious Babies. But little do *they* know that Hilary Starfessed, unscrupulous executive manager of Tin Type Hall, is recruiting help from (Mozart, Berlioz, Wagner) in a bid to forestall a visit from Dr Cary, the only man who can approach Tin Type Hall. Now read on.)

'You have lost weight,' says Hilary Starfessed,

standing in the entrance to my cell, sipping a glass of sherry.

'I haven't eaten,' I reply. 'These damn films make me lose weight.'

(Showing at the moment is Errol Flynn as the Scarlet Pirate or something similar. The soundtrack is a blur of badly-recorded shouts and screams, mingled with the dull gritty blast of cannon fire. I have a piercing headache, and can hardly bear to look at the screen.)

'We're doing all we can for you, you know. It's an ill wind that blows nobody to the end of the rainbow. You must appreciate that we're sacrificing as much time to assist you as is feasible. We're very overworked people.'

'I'm sure you are. I know you are, you've told me. But all I want to do is ...' I pause, biting my lip and looking down at my scruffy shoes.

'Yes?' asked Hilary, swilling sherry round in his blown-out cheeks. 'All you want to do is what? Escape? Is it that you want to escape? I hardly think so Mr Crisp. In fact, I'd lay money on it.'

'I'm not saying anymore,' I tell him dully. 'Just go away and leave me alone.'

'I'm trying to accommodate you, Mr Crisp. But at this moment I am afraid it is impossible for me to leave. You have a visitor. A friend of ours is coming to see you.'

I walk up to the concrete wall where the film is showing and stand against it. The gray and silver patterns flicker over my back and hands, translating me into old two-dimensional movie characters. I feel completely drained – had a visitor to my silver cell once. Last whispers of 1910 melt in my fingers and scar my face. I feel 100 years old, the dry wind of London moaning in the chimneys of Lots Road Power Station. Drop in sometime, old friend. How much does it cost to keep eyeing me. The poisoned gray cyanide of the city, and the last prowl of tape-recorders. Is that you John Remorse. Is that you Dr Cary.

I feel the room is full of cats. But when I turn to look it is empty, except for the films, accept for Hilary Starfessed standing in the doorway with his glass of sherry, smiling at me blandly and nodding.

(The love affair. Just telling you on that deserted street corner in Streatham, fingers interlocked for the last time, the last kiss which is nothing but pain. And finally she walks around the corner and is lost from sight, and I walk slowly to the Happy Time café and a cup of tea.)

'Your visitor,' announces Hilary slowly, 'is a qualified psychiatrist. He is a very sympathetic man. You should get on well. His name is Szondi, Dr Paul Szondi.'

'I've never heard of him,' I mutter, turning and sitting down again on my hard concrete bed. 'I don't want to see him. Please give me some peace and quiet.'

Hilary Starfessed ignores me. He dips the tip of his little finger in his sherry glass and sucks it.

'Dr Szondi is coming to give you a test. It will help us evaluate your position here. There are suggestions that you have some sort of intentions as far as Tin Type Hall is concerned ...'

'It's nonsense,' I growl. 'You're all mad. I want nothing to do with the place.'

Hilary grins. 'There's no need to be belligerent. Now personally, I don't believe you have any evil wishes as far as Tin Type Hall is concerned. I believe you, I mean it. But you realise as executive manager I have to placate everybody, and there are members on my board who are disturbed about you. This is only a routine enquiry.'

(I am lying on what appears to be a medical trolley. Above me there is nothing by gray. I may be blind. I cannot move my arms. It seems as though my head is detached from my body. There are soft whispers to one side of me, but I am unable to move my head to see what they are. I cannot focus my mind. I am lying here in strange vacant limbo listening to the quiet sinister whispers of Tin Type Hall.

Someone is approaching on careful feet. I can hear them breathing as they breathe over me. The breath smells slightly of medical alcohol and peppermints. I try to see who it is, but there seems to be a gray bandage over my eyes. The breathing continues for a few moments, then recedes.

Eventually there is a slight bumping movement behind me, as though someone is taking hold of the trolley. Then there is a rolling sensation, and the uniform gray above me begins to shift. It appears I am being wheeled away from my cell and along a corridor. There is silence, except for the slight whirring sound of the wheels.

'You must realise,' says a distant voice, 'that he is in a very serious condition. Treat him with great care.'

'Of course,' comes a disembodied reply from another direction.

Perhaps I am unconscious. Perhaps I have been involved in an accident. Could it be that I am badly burned or mutilated? Why do they have to take such care over me? Am I insane? Just telling you the dull gray light of Tin Type Hall seeps behind my eyes. Just telling you drop in sometime.)

'Ground zero minus three miles,' says a metallic voice. Up here, folks, the sky is almost black. Homing instruments of Mickey Mouse Alpha One clicking like an expensive roulette wheel. B-52 jets over barren Arctic countryside – below radar level here, by Jiminy.

'Ground zero minus two miles,' buzzes the relay. The vast bay doors revolve open, and a blast of salt-clean stratospheric air sucks into the bomb racks, spangling the machinery with ice. A group of chiffon-clad girls in a giant wedding-cake suspended from electric cables begin to shiver.

'Oh, you've never seen such a sunrise.' Could almost feel Cold Sun, whispers Mandrake the Magician in his personal jet plane as he flies with top hat and cloak over the Barrier Reef. Are you ready for Night Train. Are you ready for the Last Wind.

Arctic Sea crawls below barren on ice floes. 'Ground zero minus 900 yards.' Mickey Mouse Alpha One, its windows bright-lit against the Polar night, is alive with the sounds of New Year's Eve music and revelling. The cold thunder of the jet scratches against the sky.

'The suspects are in the house next door.' 'Ground zero minus 100 yards.' 'There is no house next door.' Just remember the mind's representative as the frozen brain of Motherwell the Everlasting Electric Cake touches with lethal weapon the hand of danger is around.

'Contact,' says a luminous panel on computer Jayne Mansfield.

Brighton is suddenly turned inside out, white on white is negative bomb flash. The Dome fades, the Pavilion fades, Carlton Hill is white-hot with incandescent sparks. The streets begin to crawl with radio-active heat, and the leaves are burned into old newsprint. Dead birds drop from the air in soft flocks. 1930s musical cast sprinkles into star ash and dusts his cheeks.

'Get out of town,' last message from choking computer. The sea is thick with rancid scum, and iridescent fish bob to the surface. A lonely man in a glowing wheelchair sucks at the glistening bones of his fingers. The Last Wind howls hot and heavy over the hotel roofs.

And from street to street in a wicker coffin on wheels, news photographer Ron Holland of the Evening Waistcoat. He takes flash pictures at every corner, smoking a Senior Service and humming to himself the soft tune of 'Lilli Bolero'. (Just remember the mind's representative.)

Paul Szondi arrives at my cell door carrying a large brown Gladstone bag that looks like an old spaniel. He looks very white and unwell, and his wavy blond hair is thick with dandruff. He smiles vaguely at Hilary Starfessed, pushes past him and sits down next to me on my concrete bunk.

'I'll give you a test,' he says shyly. 'I've got it all here in my bag. It shouldn't take long.'

Szondi at this time is plagued by an enormous tape-worm. He caught it on one of his rock-scrambling trips in the Dolomites, and since then it has grown in his intestines until it is nearly 100 feet long – white and blind and greasy.

The tape-worm is growing hungrier and hungrier, and Szondi has to have a full meal six times a day to keep alive. Once the worm poked its viscous head out of his mouth and bit at a corned-beef sandwich he was holding in his hand.

At night he can feel it slithering around his insides. When it shifts very violently, he is almost thrown out of bed. He calls it Humphrey and hates it. He had an offer from Workman Bill and the Famous Ear to blow it out of him with dynamite, but he declined.

Szondi Test, invented by Paul's namesake, is a vague and ambiguous method of determining psychotic characteristics. A series of photographs is shown to the patient, without him knowing they are pictures of schizophrenics, homosexuals, catatonics and neurotics.

The patient is asked which character he would like to travel with in a railway carriage. Szondi theorised that there was either attraction or repulsion between people of similar natures, and therefore the patient's choice of photograph would give an indication of his own psychological state.

Paul opens his withered old Gladstone bag and takes out a grubby set of faded photographs. He hands them to me without a word, then takes a banana sandwich from the case and begins to chew it as he watches me.

'What do you want me to do?' I ask dully, without even looking at the pictures.

'Choose one,' says Szondi, tapping a pale finger on the photos. 'See which face you like the best, and tell me which one it is. Imagine you're on a railway journey with them – a long one. Who would you prefer to sit next to?'

I shuffle numbly through the prints. You must realise that there hasn't been time to locate real schizophrenia and paranoids, so the photographs are of Mandrake the magician, Steve Reeves, Humphrey

Bogart, Daliah Lavi and Nubar Gulbenkian. The photographs are very poor quality, and it is almost impossible to distinguish the features in them.

('Choose one' tapping a pale tape-worm as he watches me. A vague and ambiguous method of catatonics. He had an offer to get out of town, but was reluctant to travel. Withered Gladstone photograph just telling you a poor quality 'what do you want me to do'. He kept eyeing me, showing no more emotion than Mandrake the Banana Sandwich.)

So I take out a photograph at random and give it back to him. Szondi, sandwich in one hand, looks at it carefully, and looks over its quivering edge at me.

'Does that satisfy you?' I ask in a brittle voice.

Szondi's tongue digs around inside his lower lip, chasing banana. He swallows and shakes his head and nods and coughs and blinks all at the same time. Behind him, fat and smiling Hilary Starfessed peers over his shoulder and sips sherry.

'Just telling you, I'm a little disturbed,' says Paul Szondi. 'In fact, I'm very disturbed.'

He gathers up the rest of his pictures, and throws them along with his half-eaten sandwich into the Gladstone bag. He bows vaguely to Starfessed, and then hurries out. I sit back against the hard wall and close my eyes.

'We're doing everything we can,' grunts Starfessed, and leaves too. 'Tokyo Joe' is appearing on screen for the third time.

The dour smell of dock leaves and burdock is very strong in the cool, dim evening. We are in Essex, in a field not far from Earl's Colne, and it is a week since Jack Beauregard was assassinated in the Haymarket. The moon is already quite high in the sky, and the trees are beginning to darken.

Over the grass, in a straggling line, come 20 little boys in Scout uniform. They are chattering to themselves like birds, and each of them carries a large rucksack. The clank of enamel mugs can be heard over the distant meadows.

At their head, in khaki shorts and a floppy green beret, leaning on a knobbly wooden stave as he walks, is Motherwell the Everlasting Executioner. One of his main cover-stories is being a scoutmaster, and at the moment he is on a week's camp with the Third Mandrake group.

'Sir,' pipes up a small fellow in NHS glasses and shorts that come down to his shins, 'Sir, have we much longer to go, sir?'

Motherwell gives him an ice-pick stare. 'What's the matter, dear, are your shorts chafing? Remember the Scout Law, can't you? A scout must be brave, or something more like it, if my memory serves me. Get back into line, Figgins love, or I'll do you an injury.'

'Yes, sir. Sorry, sir.'

Finally, Motherwell halts, and drives his stave into the grass. The little group are in the middle of a wide fallow field, surrounded on all sides by black and sinister oak trees. There is the smell of a stream nearby, and the evening air is laced with mosquitoes and gnats.

'Right, you sweet little crew, pitch your tents,' calls Motherwell in his falsetto voice. There is a harsh answering hoot from a nighthawk.

Soon the field is dotted with eleven white camping tents, showing up luminous in the dark. Motherwell delegates two of the ugliest boys to dig a latrine, and gets the others to light a camp fire so that he can have some cocoa.

He sits on a log, his legs narrow and blue in his shorts, cursing and muttering and sipping at his mug. The wan, faces of the little Scouts are flushed with the heat of the fire.

After a cigarette, he gets up, stretching and scratching his bony ribs. 'Right, time for us to go to bye-byes, I think, honeysuckles,' he says.

An older scout whom he recognises as Burfutt, leader of the Pansy Troop, suddenly raises his hand.

'What's the matter with you?' snaps Motherwell. 'You're not in school now. You know where it is, lovely, you helped dig it!'

'It's not that, sir,' says the boy seriously. 'It's just that you've forgotten prayers tonight.'

Motherwell stares at Burfutt with glittering eyes, and for a moment some of the scouts think he is going to strike him. But his face gradually thaws into a bitter smile, and he places his hand on the scout's shoulder. His fingers gently massage the boy's woodcraft badge.

'Burfutt, Burfutt, why persecuteth thou me?' he whispers. 'I'm running a group of scouts, and they're the dirtiest-minded bunch of juvenile atheists I've ever met. I'm not a vicar, darling. If you want to have a church service in the middle of a sodden field at half-past eleven at night, that's up to you. But I'm going to hit the sack.'

Without another word, he turns away and disappears into his tent. The scouts, silent and tired, walk back to their respective tents and climb into their sleeping bags. By midnight, except for the occasional tousled visitor to the earth-smelling latrine, they are all asleep.

But of course, Motherwell does not sleep. On the silent feet of a nervous and practised gunman, he prowls all night from tent to tent with a large pair of infra-red glasses on. His thin face peers through the slits in the tents, insect-like in the spectacles, and ogles the sleeping scouts. His breath comes in thin, taut whines.

(Just remember the Programme of Sliced Man. The wires of Tin Type Hall hum and chirrup in the electric-filled sky. It is impossible to trace the city. The night grows darker, and the signs of Charlotte Street indicate today the day. The Captain of Kodak passes through walls and factories, his phosphorescent film at the ready. Just telling you 'drop in sometime'.)

A gray and uncompromising morning finds Motherwell the Everlasting Executioner lighting his first cigarette from the Scouts' camp fire. He coughs phlegm into his handkerchief, and sits miserable with goose-pimple thighs while the boys prepare their breakfast.

'Get on with it, damn you,' he says bitterly. 'This is a camp, not a Cordon Bleu.'

Silver mist lies on the grass like fog of old 1920's movies. It's the Gray Cold that is turning Motherwell's lips to ice and freezing his bony fingers. He knows it and whispers: 'Could almost feel Cold Sun', as the first rooks shriek in the trees, and dawn fades though the fields.

The Scouts sit shivering on their sleeping-bags, chewing half-cooked sausages and cold baked beans. Motherwell scans them with his meat trader's eyes and wonders desperately how he is going to keep them occupied for a week. He has many disgusting alibis and this is the worst. He smiles and lights another cigarette.

But finally they raise a soup-stained Union Jack over the Essex field, and Motherwell sends them on various pointless errands, like collecting oak leaves, or observing squirrels, or calculating the voltage of the electrified fence around the meadow.

Then he goes back to his tent, flops down on his camp-bed, and reads Health and Efficiency Magazines until it's time for lunch.

It's over lunch that he first spots Charlie Bowdre and his Travelling Victorian Naughties. He is sitting on a log, chattering Scouts gathered about him, munching spotted dick, when a small group of men appear from behind a damp clump of trees.

Motherwell lays his enamel plate in the grass, and stands up. The men can obviously see him, but they do not wave. Instead, they begin unrolling a bright purple tent from a large sack. They erect it unsteadily, and then disappear inside. Motherwell rubs his chin and stares at it for a long time.

'Sir, is that another Scout troop, sir?' asks Burfutt, leader of the Pansy troop. Motherwell looks down at him with an icy expression and shakes his head.

'No, Burfutt, they are not Scouts at all,' he replies. 'I'd trouble all you lads to avoid that particular purple tent. There may be some trouble, dears, and we don't want that.'

Without another word, he takes his plate to the fire, and scrapes his spotted dick into it. It falls with a flop, and sizzles. Then he walks over to his tent, and emerges with his big black Luger in hand.

As though on wheels, Motherwell glides across the morning grass. The Scouts watch him nervously as he fades through the hedge and re-appears in the next field. His fingers and teeth are glowing with strange phosphorescence. Just telling you there is cold anger in his meat trader's eyes. He is humming as he goes his favourite tune, 'Jeannie with the Light Brown Hair.'

Charlie Bowdre, short and stocky with saliva on his moustache, pushes back the flap of the purple tent as Motherwell arrives. He smiles broadly and holds out his hand.

Motherwell stares at him coldly, a luminous green finger against his nostrils. His lethal weapon is fused to his hand, and pulses with electric anticipation.

'Hallo, friend,' says Bowdre cheerily. 'Nice to see you doing some good for a change. I've decided to give your little lads a treat. This tent here contains the most erotic delights since the Taj Mahal. Care to come in and take a look?'

Motherwell doesn't move. The light of the early-morning sky is so hard and bright that you can hardly see him against the negative trees. 'Drop in sometime, the most erotic tent.'

'Come on friend,' calls Bowdre again. 'Let bygones be bygones. Come in and see the snappy entertainment I've got lined up for you. Baden-Powell wouldn't approve, but the last I heard he was dead. Fancy a good time, hey?'

'You've made a mistake this time, Mr Bowdre,' whispers Motherwell coldly.

Bowdre shrugs and smiles, his red explosive face cracked from ear to ear. 'That's for you to judge friend. Approve the goods first.'

'I tell you, you've made a mistake, Mr Bowdre,' repeats the Everlasting Bygones.

Bowdre moves forward, but it's his last move. Motherwell's pistol crackles over the silver field, and he's down, with his face in the whispering wires, and a slow stain of purple leaking across his cheek. There's a cold breeze, and his veins melt and shift into gray transparencies, Charlie Bowdre fading into the old Tom Mix character of ancient movies. A blur of dusty soundtrack, 'Sweet Sue' seeps into the meadow the colour of cold tea, and he's gone.

Motherwell's Luger whistles three times, like a man calling an old dog. The purple tent sags and collapses, guy ropes and poles falling into a tangle. The canvas is beaten as three farm-girls, their big white buttocks wobbling like blancmange, battle their way out of the purple folds. Motherwell laughs, a piping, insect laugh, as though his throat were lined with black hairs.

(But you know there's a shivering in the air, a dull clotted outline in cold morning. And a disembodied cackle like the Cheshire Cat – a smile appears, watery against the hedgerow, and slips away in herringbone airwaves.)

'Remorse!' cries Motherwell, suddenly scared. 'Remorse – is that you?'

'Just telling you he kept eyeing me,' grins John Remorse, the Serjeant of Time Film, as he sidles away across the meadows of Earl's Colne.

This is the movie case – last seen in rusty canisters. Insoluble to police and their agents – they just haven't got the knowledge of sick equipment. They trace their metal fingers over the magnetic evidence, but there's no trace of Motherwell, no trace of the dying Scouts, no trace of the Last Wind as it howls and sucks in the solemn chimneys of Lots Road Power Station.

When are you going to stop? When is something going to happen? Ha, ha, you may well ask. Or haven't you ever thought about being dead? I'm sorry, it's a mistake. The long sad chronicles of the Mysterious Babies still chirping on the empty rim of the galaxies. They're his, the Mysterious Babies – they belong to Jack Beauregard, the Eater of Cities. The Last Wind blows them across the dusty railway and into the deep swaying grass. A train ticket to Victoria, I never took the journey back, wanted to stay in Bridget Segrave's flat the rest of my life, just talking, or occasionally altering the position of the furniture (the black chaise longue is by the wall now, and four flower-covered chairs are in a chatty bunch), or even just standing by the window, looking down pensively on the passing traffic of SW5. These are my Mysterious Babies – film-like sequences of (running upstairs with that hotel smell in my nose, or that day standing 11:00am outside Baker Street Station worried about nothing). And so what are you going to do? Just walk the grainy streets of London, taking notice of the city that nobody sees any longer, the Golden Egg sign that's broken, flickering yellow Morse messages of 'Tin Type Hall' to the street, the grimy piece of wrapping paper that cartwheels past Selfridges in the city wind, the silent evenings of Kensington Gardens and the dull mornings of the Albert Memorial. 'I'm not a prince – I'm a bygone.' Oh yes, it's a mistake. Ask Dr Cary, the only man who can approach Tin Type Hall. He'll say, in a voice as dry as leaves: 'When are you going to stop? When is something going to happen? He kept eyeing me …' Then he'll move away on old time film of Marylebone, his throat withered in his soft check collar, waving with his Daily Express the last farewell. You remember me. I'm here. I'm talking to you now, and it's growing late. It's growing late and the clock has tricked me. The last train has left for Three Bridges. The last wind is sucking at the chimneys of Lots Road Power Station. An arc of swallows go calling across the dusty mudflats of the Thames. I'm here, I'm speaking to you. Just remember the mind's representative.

She wrote a story once, and I read it in front of the three-bar electric fire in the bedroom. It was about a young girl, quite mad, lying in a hospital. She thought she had a lover. Perhaps she had one once – but not now. The doctors and nurses were quiet and white and sympathetic. The story reminded me of Woodside Hospital, and I couldn't finish it. I kept thinking she was the same girl.

And the time came, not long after, when I knew I was growing old. I was so old that nobody recognised me. I couldn't talk to anyone any longer, because they couldn't understand what I was saying. I chatted to them about their families and their mopeds, but when I really began to speak, they just nodded and smiled and their eyes glazed and I began to think I was either hideously boring or mad. But I'm neither. I'm just old. Old and tired and having so much difficulty in keeping my eyes open.

(The Captain of Kodak lays the time negatives one on top of another, like ghostly sheets. The face blurs and transposes, and a white gloss make the eyes shift into visions of Buster Keaton on a silent railway trolley.)

I'm thinking of making a run for it. They're closing in on all sides, the Mysterious Babies. They're all around me now, and Motherwell the White-Faced Executioner is out loose in the streets with his dream gun and his floating feet. A run will have to come soon. Down the stairs, and out of the difficult door, and across the car park between the Embassy Cinema and the Chinese restaurant. They mustn't get me. They scare me to death. They're all around, burbling and whispering, and I'm too tired and frightened to go on.

(It is so hot and humid that the sweat drops off the ends of my fingers like pearls. It's night, and we've been walking through the city for nearly four hours, a guided tour of Chinatown by Mr Lim. He's taken us through the markets and the slums, and the urine-smelling backstage of wayang. I'm not footsore, just excited with my new life. We turn a corner and we're in Orchard Street again, and it's alive with lights and the odour of noodles.)

'*Où se trouve* Batman? *Où se trouve* Eddie Constantine?'

'I've seen a butcher show more feeling.'

Jack Beauregard's first contact with The Ugly Family is at a wedding. Two acquaintances of his – a six-foot-nine Jewess who runs a gloomy boarding-house, and William Turner, an excommunicated GP from Belfast – are getting married in a Kensington church (St Charlotte of the Clothespegs). The Jewess, Dolores Shallott, has insisted on marrying in white, even though both she and William Turner have totalled at least 13 weddings and divorces between them, and Dolores has an oily middle-aged son who looks like Clark Gable (the green flicker of old movies).

So it is that Jack Beauregard finds himself perspiring in a right-hand pew on a humid Saturday afternoon, crammed onto a corner by waves of relatives who are all Ascot hats and dentures, with a mutilated hymnbook and a shaving cut that drips blood on to his collar.

The bride is so eager to get married that she arrives 10 minutes early, and stands at the back of the church in her white veil, like the Phantom of the Opera. Her 81-year old father, in a blue suit and brown shoes, keeps lifting the lid off the font and spitting into it.

The choirboys (whom Jack saw arrive only a few seconds before the wedding, racing on battered old death's-head bicycles and wearing grubby windcheaters) at last finish their song. Then the organist slides through a swelling chord and launches into 'Here Comes The Bride'. Dolores and father, two of her little sons in kilts, and two sweaty bridesmaids in pink satin, walk unsteadily up the aisle,

William Turner joins her as she approaches, and grins. He is very drunk on liqueur cognac. He is wearing the uniform of a captain of the Cunard Fleet, with 'Coldstream Guards' on his epaulettes. There is a dry little fusillade of coughs from the relatives.

Another rainbow burst of music, and the vicar springs out of the vestry, wearing a glittering silver cassock and Union Jack sunglasses. (It is the same vicar who, months later, is to officiate at the dismal funeral of Charlie Bowdre. As you can gather, he is a bit of a character.)

'Good afternoon, ladies and gentlemen and dearly beloved,' he grins. He has a dog-collar that lights up when he presses a bulb. He flashes a rather old joke about the honeymoon across the church in Morse. Nobody laughs.

'This wedding is brought to you by courtesy of the diocesan authorities and the makers of sacramental wines and biscuits,' he announces brightly.

'Now a lot of rubbish is talked about marriage, especially by people who are married. I know – my wife keeps talking about it, and she's married. A lot of people say that marriage is outdated, and that young people expect too much out of it.

'I don't know what I expected out of it, but I seem to have got what, by the grace of God, I had coming to me. Never mind – put a sugar-bag over the face, I always say, and you can't tell the difference.

'Actually, marriage probably is outdated. I mean – cut out marriage and the divorce rate will drop 100 percent. But you two old birds obviously won't make too much demand on each other. Look after the bedsprings, I say, and the home will look after itself.

'Well, you've been married so many times before; I won't bore you by going into the details. You probably know it better than I do. So please consider yourselves man and wife, and we'll go along and sign the register.'

There is a rustle of disapproval through the congregation, but the Silver Vicar has already ushered Dolores and William into the vestry to sign the book. Jack Beauregard, the Eater of Cities, is one of the witnesses, and his name appears in the same back-sloping scrawl as in the register at Chelsea College, in purple ink.

(The Captain of Kodak is waiting outside in the drizzle to freeze the wedding group into dull gray pictures which are later either lost or forgotten. He uses an infra-red film, and the nylon-clad bride appears to be standing in the middle in the overgrown churchyard dressed in nothing but a ghostly suspender-belt. The day is sticky, in spite of the rain.)

The Ugly Family – considering they are so very ugly – are extremely dear to social circles. Perhaps it is because they are all kind and sympathetic, and will lend a cauliflower ear, well paprikaed with spots, to any troubled friends.

They are very well known for what they call their 'Angstfests' – when anybody with anything from full-scale catatonia to a congenital disability to hold canapés without dropping them on their shoes, is invited down for the weekend to talk it out of their system. The Family have a very large manor-house near East Grinstead – previously the boarding house where Gordon Casper lived. During an 'angst' weekend, it is packed with guests, and many of them forget to leave – wander about the corridors with pale faces for years, waiting for the dinner-gong.

The Ugly Family do not appear to be actually related to anybody (except of course themselves). Claiming kinship with them would create serious difficulties during the Season. No mother would feel at ease about surrendering Jennifer, diary and dowry, to a man who might have Ugly blood lurking somewhere in his veins.

'It would be a disaster, my dear, of catastrophic proportions,' says Mrs Cholmondeleigh-Brygges at a Norfolk ball, 'if Jennifer found herself producing a string of nasty little dwarves.'

'Judging by her current escorts, darling, you seem to have done that for her,' replies a scrawny Viscountess with buttocks like the Tay Bridge disaster (1879).

But the Ugly Family take everything very jovially in their stride, and appear everywhere in a big green charabanc, driven by Peter Hostess of the Big Bang Remedy Co, and specially fitted with one-way ambulance windows to protect (their ripened sense of ugliness).

There are at least 20 of them, and they are never seen separately. Reporter A14 knows only three personally – Enox, the head of the Family; Margaret, his wife; and Pin, who could be either male or female, but seems on the whole to wear full-length ball gowns.

It is impossible to get to know the Family intimately. They all wear papier-mâché masks of comic-strip characters (Mickey Mouse, The Green Hornet, Blondie and Dagwood) and each morning there is a General Post with these before breakfast, so that the same mask is never worn by the same person two days running.

In fact – since they are never seen without their masks – it is only a matter for conjecture whether they are ugly at all. But a window-cleaner who was working on their manor-house (Chez Bergerac) late last January, and who saw Margaret Ugly in the bath, says: 'She looked like a bloody old bit of butcher's meat – all chewed up and covered with muslin. I thought they was soaking a side of bacon at first.' (They might have been.)

The Ugly Family arrive at the wedding just as the guests are dispersing to the reception in the nearby church hall. Their garden-green charabanc comes to a shuddering halt, and they clamber out and stand in a bunch, all with painted inane grins on their masks.

There liaison officer is a tubby, but quite normal-looking man in glasses. He walks up to Reporter A14 and gives him a slightly sweaty handshake. Reporter A14 (now disguised as Jack Beauregard) nods to the still-smiling Family and asks: 'Who are they?'

'They're very well known,' replies the liaison man breathlessly, poking his glasses further back on his nose. 'They're the Ugly Family. Great supporters, incidentally, of the Evening Waistcoat. They've come to the wedding as friends.'

'Friends of whom?'

'Friends of each other. They don't know anybody else here, I'm afraid. But they are extremely fond of weddings. They saw this one and just couldn't resist it.'

Jack Beauregard turns to stare at the ill-assorted Family in the churchyard. Enox, the head of the Family, is talking very loudly about Malcolm Muggeridge. From behind a mauve and expressionless Batman mask, he is booming: '– an ephemeral man – a fad in philosophy's clothing – an enfant terrible in his second childhood.'

(Eric Goodbody – the liaison man – introduces Beauregard to the Family. 'This is Reporter A14 of the Evening Haberdashery,' he says. 'He is standing in for Jack Beauregard, the Eater of Cities, or he may be Jack Beauregard. I'm not sure which.')

Enox growls cheerfully: 'You're from the Waistcoat, hey? I like your cartoon page!'

Reporter A14 replies coldly: 'I don't write the cartoon page.'

Enox – head and shoulders above A14 – yet with a curious lack of substance – an empty black suit that has somehow become inflated and animate. ('He has an orgasm every time he sees the Michelin Man.')

'What sort of work d'you do then?' he asks, not in the least put out.

'I'm a reporter. A special correspondent on Tin Type Hall. A chaser-round, a doorstep-job man. I've written one paragraph in three weeks and I'm gradually breaking into bits.'

Enox's eyes glitter behind the papier-mâché cut-outs. He rests a gray-gloved hand on my arm – a hand that leaks dust and smells of old motor cars.

'Now – that's most interesting,' he breathes.

'What is?'

'The expression you used – "I'm gradually breaking into bits". Could you explain it more? Go into more detail?'

I shake my head. The stifling weather has given me a headache, and I am beginning to feel slightly bilious.

'I don't know – it's only a phrase. What am I supposed to say? I don't see what you're getting at.'

Enox clasps his hand behind his back and bows his head thoughtfully. He rubs his cardboard chin and says in a level voice: 'You say you're a correspondent of Tin Type Hall?'

'Correct. For nearly three years now. I know it as well as anybody will ever know it.'

'Have you ever heard of Motherwell – also known as The Everlasting Executioner?'

'Of course. I know the Tin Type Hall hierarchy as of last week. It may have altered since then, of course.'

'And do you know of John Remorse, the Serjeant of Time Film? And have you heard of The Programme of Sliced Man?'

(The scene shifts and merges very rapidly. We are now in an old Ford Thames van, driving through Whitechapel. Someone is talking in a very indistinct voice about football – the World Cup or something similar. I cannot feel my hands because of the grey.)

'Here he approaches the ice cream seller. "What would you like – cream or chocolate?" she asks in a sort of dirty voice. And all at once "it's as if splinters of black coal spread through the ice cream. Can such ice-cream exist?"

'Or a sudden loud ringing at the door "and the ringing rolled over and over and my fingers felt something cold and there was a salty taste in my mouth ..."

'Or lunch in a restaurant, the taste of which varies with the music, ("probably they're playing specially to improve the taste") and then quite suddenly noises on the roof where they are repairing the roofing – "and, all at once the lunch tasted horrible, completely spoiled" ...'

These records of synaesthesia from the files of A R Luria, the Russian psychologist. Also neatly stored away on pink cards in the vast and comprehensive files on Tin Type Hall, where even now John Remorse, Agent Manhole Section Drop, is preparing the Programme of Sliced Man.

(Reminds me of a garden fete, three years ago, organised by a rich financier who for the sake of argument we shall call Sir Humphrey Z------, when a beauty queen arrived in a helicopter to the cheering of vast crowds. She placed a magnificent trophy on a plinth, but the cup was so light that it blew away in the summer wind, and rolled across the lawns ...')

The programme commences with Dreams. John Remorse in his green-lit surgery in Tin Type Hall controls the association blocks which divide and cross London. His fingers are quiet and businesslike as they stir and fade over the formulae of illusion. The wires buzz and hum, and the electricity of the day meet under my skin.

The Dream is that you have murdered the driver of the bus. He falls and slides out of his cab on the road. You are surrounded by angry passengers, one of them a huge and fearsome man with a rolled-up newspaper. You cannot fight them, for your pistol has faded into your own pointing fingers.

Or you have been sent to a monastery – an enormous, rich, warm building. You meet the son of the Abbot, who invites you into the drawing-room for a drink. There is a waiter there with a tray of Scotch eggs, and you take one, only to find that it is dripping with a watery anchovy sauce.

The Abbot's son leads you upstairs, and you leave splashes of light brown sauce on the carpet. He takes you into his father's bedroom, which smells of eiderdown and mothballs, and kneels down and opens the wardrobe mirror.

'This is a masturbation scene from a new film,' you think suddenly, and you are running down the corridor, still leaving droplets of sauce.

There is a mirror beside you, and on the inside of the glass, as though in a polished cage, a white mouse is flying. Its pink nose is up against the glass, and its tail and hind legs are blurred, like a humming-bird.

You are screaming for help, but your voice is hoarse and useless. And then the Serjeant of Time Film withdraws his silver hands, and the Dreams are swallowed back into the wires, and they dwindle into the cathode fuses of his plan.

You see, it is quite silent. The Programme of Slice Man throbs softly over the metallic darkness of London. It prowls the streets on the footsteps of Motherwell. The Dream is that you have called it so light. The wires of a flying film leads you inside. Its pink nose is surrounded by angry music, but your voice withdraws like a watery falls and slides.

'But you remember each other inside my skin.'

'He kept eyeing me … Is that you?'

'Just telling you he was a man of conscience. He showed no more emotion.'

'Here he approaches the thin dark nape of gas.'

I return to my office the following day, tired and gritty, to find that there is a message on my desk from Samuel Baptist. He insists that I contact him at once, and says: 'These are the records of "drop in sometime."'

4

but you remember each other inside my skin

The love affair is suddenly over, and I am driving on my own again, and there is no one beside me on the seat of my summery car.

'How do you feel?' says Rufus, and for once he is genuinely concerned, and he offers me a cigarette, which he seldom does.

I am not too upset. I think I have done the best thing. I feel a little older and a little more nostalgic, because you miss the places that were associated with your affair almost as much as you miss the person you once loved. But, in a way, I feel free.

'I was very fond of her,' I tell him. He has his back to the window, and the early sun is burning into his beard. He nods and gives a little grin, as if that will be helpful.

'I know, oh smarting Lothario,' he chuckles.

(But you remember it is May, and it should be raining. It was raining in Singapore the night I left her in the noisy tropical dark. Warm spatters at first, and the frogs were bellowing from the marshes. Then so heavily that the storm drains over-gorged. I was driven from Tanglin to Changi by an old Malayan, who asked me how he could send his sons to Oxford.)

Of course, it is sad. But I am still young, and there are other women. One night in Buenos Aires, a hot still night with a sudden sunset. That will be the time. If I'm ever in Buenos Aires.

I am on my way to Tooting. It's evening now. You can tell the time by Garner Ted Armstrong on Radio London, pressing his way through The World Tomorrow with his usual great urgency.

He is saying as I turn out of Queenstown Road into Clapham Common: '… and let's face it, have you ever seen an UGLY sunset?'

No, Garner Tea, I have never seen an ugly sunset. But I have seen an ugly woman and an ugly tree. I have seen the fear of Jack Beauregard as he runs across The Last Street with his hands to his head, waiting for the lethal whistles of Tin Type Hall.

(The Raffles Hotel, Singapore. I was sitting at a low glass-topped table when she walked in. It was a monsoony night soon after Christmas, 1965. We were going on a tour of Chinatown with Mr Lim Kim Guan of the Straits Times. We were drinking beer and the Raffles Hotel was The Last Outpost of colonialism. I remember a fish tank quietly bubbling in the corner, a bamboo bead curtain.)

What more do you want? What more can you ask for? And it's questions of this sort that require no answer that I'm saying as I turn left into Tooting Broadway past the traffic lights and police boxes. Doctor Who, you made it here at last.

Samuel Baptist is waiting for me at Amen Corner. I draw the car into the kerb, and he quickly steps in. He smells of Tabac, and has to catch his breath for a moment. I notice that he isn't looking well.

'What's new?' I ask him as we turn into Welham Road. It's a dull suburban street with nothing to distinguish it but Rosa Bassett School and a few stumpy plane trees.

'It's very urgent,' pants Samuel. 'Something has gone very wrong and I've been trying all evening to find out what. Turn left here.'

'Wrong? Do you mean at Tin Type Hall? Is Beauregard all right?'

'Oh, he's all right. He's still very well in with them. It's just that there's no sign of Black Rod and no sign of Hilary Starfessed. This is why I want to take you up to the Common. We're meeting one of our double-agents to see if we can patch up the broken link.'

We're driving along Furzedown Drive now. The streetlights are lit, but there is still a watery smear of light behind the rooftops. It's one of those still English evenings when you feel it's going to rain. The houses are neat and closed, and could be empty for all we can see.

We stop at a dismal parade of shops. There's an RACS, Co-op, a newsagent and a small haberdashers on the corner – the sort that sells 1950ish baby clothes and faded knitting patterns. Samuel gets out of the car and walks swiftly over to it.

From the car, I can see him talking with an old woman in an overcoat and headscarf. His hands are gesticulating up and down, and she is pointing towards the shop door. After a while, he bows and walks out again. He gives me a small smile as he comes across to the car.

'Everything's fixed up,' he reports. 'We're to make our way slowly to Tooting Graveney Common, and wait by the pond. The agent will approach us there.'

We set off into the darkness. The radio is playing 'We're Happy Together', and it gives me a pang. Baptist is humming selections from (Mozart, Hendrix, Berlioz). He is a very poised man, but he is getting too old (for this sort of thing).

On the common, it's chilly, and the wind's beginning to blow. The bushes and grass have the squat, deserted look of all parks at night. The pond is a luminous white space. A duck furrows it, and the banks are full of shadow.

'Cigarette?' says Baptist, and we smoke.

The fragments of smoke are lost in the thickening gloom. I begin to wonder what I am doing here at all. Behind the trees, a row of sodium lights are flickering gently in the wind. I try not to think about her, but as you know it's very hard.

All those days of life together, you see, and here I am standing in a cold park waiting for a double-agent. Love is always just over. Even the chill reminds me of a frosty day we spent together in Woburn Square. And in fact from where I am standing I can see the sports-ground railings where we leaned one clear blue day and talked of love.

(There is a low call. It's real. I am suddenly back at today and now, and a tall figure is approaching us across the grass. Baptist's cigarette sparks red as he throws it away. I do the same, with the practised flick of a man who has long grown used to the idea of being shot at.)

'Who's that?' says Baptist.

'Not to worry, governor. Park keeper,' grunts a voice.

I almost believe it for a moment, but the voice is wrong, and my scalp tingles freezing cold, and I want to shout to Samuel but the words are suddenly clogged with darkness. I can already see that Samuel is moving away, he's doing it so slowly, I can watch the film-like blur of his arms and legs as he dives and scrambles out of range.

Those long bird-like whistles are all around. They seem to blot out my vision. I am away across the grass in heavy battling leaps. The frosty air snorts into my lungs and screws up my ribs. The whistles die, and I can't run any more, but I keep jogging sweatily towards the main road where I left the car.

It's still there, under the lamp post, with a dull patina of fog on it. I throw myself in, gun the engine and drive at almost 60mph to the corner of Furzedown Drive. I brake, looking wildly around for Samuel, but he's nowhere to be seen. I drive off towards Mitchan Lane, my hands tight on the steering wheel, tensing nervously at every passing car.

(Another abortive mission. The plot is becoming too complicated. It should have worked out, but there's too much danger around. The sky is singing tonight the night. Only a cover charge, but you remember the Sad Vendor of Willow Street.)

'It's you,' says Samuel softly, silhouetted against the pond.

The tall figure comes closer, and raises a hand in greeting. I move forward to join them, and reach for another cigarette. These evening meetings are like small slices of the Cold War. The double-agent is stooped and older than I thought when he first approached.

'Tom, this is Arthur Smith. Arthur The Laughter Smith because of his famed cackle. Isn't that right,

Arthur?'

Arthur nods, and has a broad Wiltshire accent. 'That's what they say. I'm from Swindon. How do you do, Tom. I know you, I don't need surname.'

Having exchanged hellos, we walk quickly across the park to where I left the car. It has a thin film of fog on it. Samuel gets in the back seat, and Arthur sits next to me. 'Lovely bit of machinery,' he says, but not enviously.

I glance over at Arthur from time to time as we drive towards Clapham. He is a typical employee of Tin Type Hall. He has intense, near-together eyes and a short wiry haircut. His nose is pointed, with bristles of hair sticking from his nostrils. He is wearing a gray gabardine raincoat, and has a single silver ring on his right hand.

'What we're mainly concerned with,' I say, changing to third and swallowing smoke, 'is the present position of Jack Beauregard. I think everybody has suddenly realised how important that man can be.'

Arthur The Laugher nods. 'Starfessed has certainly realised it, Tom. As far as I can make out, there's quite a lot of pressure on him already. I don't know how far they've got, because Beauregard is out a lot on this Shepperton job.'

'The housing estate, you mean?'

'That's it. They don't want to arouse suspicion, especially among you lot. But I can see that they've already done so. It's a difficult situation to keep quiet, especially with security at Tin Type Hall in the mess it's in at the moment.'

Aha. We're getting at the nub of it, you see, if you follow what's happening. It's beginning for once to click into place. It's nice; it's like playing a card game with blank cards, and then slowly realising that you can tell which is which.

We're passing through Chelsea already. King's Road, Fulham Road, and it's not long before we're across the maze of traffic lights and glittering cars and on our way East into Hyde Park. I notice, as I always notice, the rotting boot in a tank of water in the Piccadilly shop front. I must find out one day how long it's been there. It's probably older than I am.

'I'll give you one piece of advice, Tom,' says Arthur as we drop him at the corner of Haymarket.

'I'm listening.'

'Watch out for John Remorse. He's the bogey in this game, son. He's the one you want to look out for, even before Motherwell. He'll spin you round until you're blind – ha ha ha ha ha ha.'

And he's gone, and Samuel and I drive on.

The story of Jack Beauregard, the Eater of 'Hold On, I'm Coming.' He's a marked man, and he knows it. He walks around with a crease in his forehead, averting his eyes from the street. They're trying to buy him off, and he knows what that means. They're selling him out all around, and he knows it's only a matter of time.

I meet him one August morning in the Amazon Tea Rooms, opposite Zion Street Baptist Chapel. It has steamy windows with Pepsi-Cola signs and a large battered juke-box. I take up typical agent position behind a potted palm and light a cigarette while sipping my coffee. The Espresso machine gurgles like a dying robot.

He's 15 minutes late, hiding his face behind his pale fingers. He sits opposite me, hands in his lap, a little out of breath, and saying nothing.

'Coffee?' I say. He shakes his head. He's not even looking at me. His fingers come up and fiddle with some sugar crumbs on the tablecloth.

'How's Shepperton going?'

'All right. Should be clear in a month. You're not supposed to know about that.'

I grimace. 'You know what your security's like at the moment. Starfessed is making a right hash of it, and we all know it.'

Beauregard looks like someone I knew a long time ago. His haunted face is familiar, and yet out of touch. A friend you once had, and yet can no longer help. I realise, not without sadness, that any offer I make him will be useless. I can't save him. I wish I could, but he's marked. Once you're marked, you're on the outside for good. No distance, no money, nothing can save you from the finish that's got to come. He's already dead, and I'm making him offers.

'The suspect is in the image next door.' (There is no image next door.)

A14 breathes smoke from his nostrils and grips Beauregard's arm. It's painfully thin under his mackintosh. The reporter says urgently: 'You know what we want. There's more than a chance in it for you.'

Beauregard (dim as a snapshot of 1910 Panama) has already accepted. There's nothing more he can do, so he does. He nods, in a strangely feminine way, like a mother of eight learning that she's pregnant again.

'We want the code, Jack,' says A14, drawing a sheaf of papers from his inside pocket. 'We've analysed the bank-note fragments that Motherwell left behind when he killed Alfred Waltz, the bank clerk. It's some kind of association-block system, we know that much. We want you to provide the rest.'

(Beauregard takes the papers, which may or may not be money. His face is engraved with nothing. His limbs flicker in long-lost movement of 'The Love Affair'.

Has he ever been in love? His eyes are no longer giving anything away. He is fading and shimmering into 35 frames per second movie character. There's nothing left for him to do. The day outside is gray and humid, and he takes the papers.)

I suddenly stop him at the Tea Rooms door, and grip his shoulder. He doesn't look round, just freezes in mid-motion. I want more than anything to say: 'Give me the bloody things back and forget it.' But of course I can't, and he shrugs and walks out of the door and down the narrow pavement of Zion Street. He turns the corner into Eastwood Street, and that's the last time I see him alive.

(She's at my elbow as I watch him go – the girl. When I turn to look at her, she's changed again. She's older, and something has happened to her. She's nearer to becoming Bridget now – I can already detect distinct similarities. She's wearing a dull dog's-tooth jacket with a light fur collar, and flat black shoes. I give her a slight smile.)

'A Man of Conscience,' she says simply, and I don't know what she means. I hope I don't know what she means. An English lecturer I never even met accused me of 'undigested first-stage stream of consciousness.' Maybe they're all telling the truth. I get into my car and I'm so tired.

'You're in a delicate position, then,' says John Remorse the Serjeant of Time Film. Starfessed nods fatly, and sips at a tall glass of rich brown wine. He is perspiring heavily, and his wispy hair is smeared around his forehead.

Remorse is wearing a shining silver suit, and his

face is hidden by large red-lensed spectacles. One lank hand rests over the arm of his chair, and in his fingers burns a cigarette. He looks oddly disarranged and spent, as though he has just made love. (This of course is not possible. He is a virgin.)

'It was all Motherwell's fault, of course. He's a messy and old-fashioned operator,' continues Remorse. Starfessed nods again. He creaks in his basket-work chair and mops his chin.

'I can see that you've taken the only way out.'

Starfessed swivels an eye at Remorse. He nods again and again. He lifts the wine-glass up and peers in at it. 'Not in the mood for Madeira,' he grunts.

'But you can't get rid of Motherwell,' persists Remorse. 'In fact, I'd like to know who CAN get rid of Motherwell. He's disarranging our security all over the place, but you can't oust him. It's one of those things you have to live with.'

Starfessed at last appears to be ready to say something. He screws his heavy buttocks into the chair, and his goitres plunge up and down like a fat swimmer at Bournemouth.

'I hired you to do a job, John,' he breathes. 'Now, I'm not telling you how to do that job. You're a Master at it. I don't like upsetting anybody, as you well know. But a stitch in time saves two in the bush.

'I know Motherwell's ballsed it up. I know I can't get rid of him. But if we can nail Beauregard instead, that'll throw the scent off just long enough for you to get in and finish the Programme. A sacrifice, if you like. A scapegoat. I like Jack, you know that. But when we've paid all this to bring you in, we don't want to abort the mission without accomplishing anything.'

Remorse may be grinning behind his scarlet

shades. 'I understand, Hilary. As I say, you've taken the only way out.'

Hilary nods decisively. 'That's it – that's all there is to it.'

Remorse is wearing a shining silver love. His face is hidden by disarranging our security. He nods again and again, and if we can nail the arm of his silver virgin. Just telling you the wires are humming today the day. 'The Greek-key version of 1910.' The Programme of Sliced Man is on tracks and we are frantically seeking the key to its code. Mysterious Babies muttering and gurgling behind what strange events of the day.

'He kept eyeing me. Just telling you he showed no more emotion than a swivelled eye ...'

Remorse of course is already on his way to his Psychedelic Brasshouse on Clapham Common. He rides a large black motorcycle, with coonskins and pennants fluttering in the gray afternoon breeze. He chugs through a football game between Clapham Rovers and Wandsworth and Balham United as though they were wax statues.

'Offside!' whistles the referee. But John Remorse is already away between the trees in a cloud of blue smoke, humming to himself the first bars of 'Lilli Bolero'.

The Psychedelic Brasshouse is reached across a stretch of south suburban waste ground, littered with pram carcasses and spare wheels. Remorse negotiates it expertly, and then parks his motorcycle against some railings. He looks around quickly through his red insect spectacles, removes his golden crash helmet, and makes off into a scrubby clump of trees.

The Brasshouse is barely visible from the nearby

railway. It is caked with verdigris and old newspapers. Remorse approaches it as a man approaches home, and lays his hand on the spherical roof. He gazes up as he waits for the door to open. It looks like rain. Across the railway, the narrow backs of slummy South London houses. A mongrel is yelping in a deserted garage lot. Piece of a toy revolver there in nettles of the alley. Over the empty streets a red white and blue kite.

There is a low, efficient hum. A circular door slides back, and silver-suited Remorse steps in. 'How much does it cost to fall through an open manhole?' 'Drop in sometime ...'

Immediately, yes, he knows he is home. Vibrant music of Jimi Hendrix slides across his face. Freakish coloured lights pop and glimmer over the bald white decor. The door closes the afternoon behind him, and he moves forward with even, assured steps.

An old man with a face like a bearded goat is swaying from the ceiling on a white fur swing. He grins toothlessly as Remorse passes by, and spits invisible tobacco juice into magnetic vacuum. Remorse raises his hand, half in greeting.

More doors slide back, one after the other, like falling knives. John Remorse the Serjeant of Time Film moves through. His suit reflects green and orange and purple. Hendrix is singing: '... 'scuse me while I kiss this guy ...' The smoke from a dozen deserted cigarettes fills the corridors.

Gordon Caspar is waiting for him in the Frogsbreath Room. This is only Remorse's nickname for it. It was installed for him by Dr Cary, a world expert on halitosis. Over 200 whirring fans are wafting the rotting breath of Hudson's Bay Eskimos into a murky arrangement of poisonous plants and dripping creepers. Remorse screws up his nose happily as he walks in.

'Hallo, Gordon,' he says cheerfully.

Caspar looks over his shoulder and grunts. He is engrossed in the Room's control panel, trying to find ventilation that is less objectionable than Eskimos. There is a wide choice. Winking green switches indicate anything from the breath of duck-billed platypuses to betel-nut chewers of Southern Assam.

'I see you're not impressed,' Remorse comments casually. 'Follow me.'

Caspar gets up with relief and shambles after his dangerous host. Nowadays he is all National Health glasses and elbowed suits. He lost his job with the Captain of Kodak after 'The Evening Bodice' had rifled his darkroom. He attempted to start up a photographic business of his own in Gaylord Smith's old flat in Dean Street, but even with pornographic pictures he was a failure. He was cautioned by the Metropolitan Police after attempting to sell 50 photographs of a Merton housewife defecating in a wood.

Remorse is now in his tasteful office. It is white, like most of the Brasshouse. But the dream effect is heightened by four dark illusory pictures at each corner – strange knotted scenes of 'The image is in the image next door'. Caspar walks round the room, staring at each of them closely, and trying not to wipe his nose on his sleeve.

'You know why you're here,' says Remorse, drumming his fingers along the top of his narrow white desk. Caspar starts slightly.

'Er … photographs. To do with photographs. I should think.'

'In a way,' says Remorse. He makes a tent of his

hands. 'But mainly to do with newspapers.'

'I'm not with you.'

'Newspapers, Gordon. The reporters. Tom Crisp, Rufus Shack, George Macfries, Ron Holland. The bloody nosey-men. That's what I've got you here for. They're becoming a pest.'

Caspar suddenly looks knowing, and sits down for the first time. He is wearing thick wrinkled socks and scuffed shoes, but he crosses his legs with confidence.

'I know what you're on about,' he grins. 'They found the fragments. Your Programme's going up the Swanee and you want me to do something about it.'

John Remorse (his scarlet spectacles shining in the impeccable white light) says nothing. He could be smiling. He swivels to and fro in his white leather chair and smiles (or doesn't smile) at nothing and nobody. His mind is a bank of information and experience. He has Caspar trussed up in circumstances already, and yet Gordon is unaware of it. What fun.

'Behind me,' says Remorse at last, indicating an invisible door, 'is the Programme Housing. It's all in there, and I'm telling you because you'll realise then how important this all is.

'This programme has been a rush job. Three days, that's all, at £45,000 a day. It's a cheap one, and it's a dangerous one. Personally I don't like it, and I only agreed to the contract because it will clear the way for another deal I have lined up.

'I don't like it because Hilary Starfessed is on the way out at Tin Type Hall. I don't like it because Motherwell's position has not been made sufficiently clear to me. And I don't like it because there are too many people involved that I'm not sure about. It was all different in China, I can warmly assure you.'

Caspar is still grinning. 'All of which, Mr Remorse, leads to what?'

(All of which, Mr Scarlet, leads to Another Deal. He could be smiling in thick wrinkled information. His mind is a Swanee of failure. He attempted to start up an invisible door. Let me remind you that this Programme has become the Last Power Station.)

Let me remind you the Cold Draught of Tin Type Hall is shuddering under the leaf-like housings of the Psychedelic Brasshouse. Let me remind you that their electro-sensitive ears are probing the daylight with a wave of improbable sound. A glowing after-image dies and fades on the screens of the city. They're worried now, and worry is dangerous. Their eyes are out; their death is out. Captain Marvel streaks blue across the imaginary skyline. Last apple gasoline of autumn. Over the roof tops, a red white and blue kite. Just telling you Tin Type Hall shifts stirs like an old Screen Monster.

Remorse has turned almost blue with fear. Gordon still hasn't realised what is happening, but his grin fades like old movie character. A biting cold makes the paint on the walls snap. The floors sparkle with crystals of ice. There is a fearsome electric blast – it's blue and searing. Remorse is running for the Programme Housing door, his breath around him in a heavy fog.

'Motherwell!' he screams. 'Motherwell! Come out of there!'

The door rolls back on a tumult of sound. The vast Housing room is flickering in hallucinogenic light. It is laced with catwalks and high-voltage cables, and coloured bands of electricity leap and crawl from metal surface to metal surface. Caspar says: 'Oh,' and sits down again. But Remorse leaps into the blazing chaos with the ferocity of a silver insect. He is wide-eyed under his orange goggles.

'Motherwell!' he yells again. 'For Christ's sake – Motherwell!'

The darkened Housing is screaming with electric noise. Remorse drops from a catwalk on to the floor, scanning the flashing wires for his enemy. He is unarmed, he is terrified, and Motherwell the Everlasting Executioner is prowling the shrieking dark with his big black weapon in hand.

Remorse scurries across to the opposite wall and clangs up a metal ladder. From above, the Housing is alive with echoes. It is impossible to see where the Executioner is. The flickers of light are blinding, and melt his eyeballs into a thousand ghosts of after-image. He gropes towards the giant control panel, shielding himself with a steel grille. The sparks bounce softly on to it, and trickle like caterpillars on to his suit.

Motherwell is waiting for him. In the dark angle behind the control console, he stands in his ancient coat, humming under the chaos of sound his favourite tune. His face is an ice pick. In his hand, he is holding a great greasy machine-gun.

'Hallo, John dear,' he pipes. 'Nice to see you again at last. It's been four years, hasn't it, amigo?'

Remorse's mouth is dragged down at the corners with shock. He stares at Motherwell through his glasses, shuddering and twitching.

'Come, sweetness, you mustn't be afraid,' says Motherwell, in an amused tone. A crackling fork of electricity seems to blot out his face for a moment – white and overexposed.

'Don't touch me,' whispers Remorse. It's all he

can say.

'That's unfriendly,' shrugs Motherwell. 'In fact, a lot of people are being rather unfriendly these days. Can't say I find it very nice at all. I mean, look at you and fatty Starfessed.'

'You don't know about that – you can't,' breathes Remorse.

'Don't I?' Motherwell replies coquettishly, sucking in his cheeks. 'If I left all my security to (Mozart, Berlioz, Wagner) at Tin Type Hall, charmer, I'd be out of a job quicker than you can say Aubrey Beardsley. I know what's happening, ducky, and I know what to do about it.'

Without warning, he fires a rapid burst at a tall rack of steel shelves across the Housing. Remorse, without a sound, drops to his knees. Motherwell knows what he wants, and there is no stopping him.

John Remorse is dramatic, but he's a professional and a good loser. He shuts his eyes against the searing crackle of light, and waits for what he knows will happen.

It's the Eidetic Image Bank that Motherwell is after. Stored in the metal racks are thousands of time-film tracks – almost a third of John Remorse's total stock. It's the armoury of the Serjeant of Time Film – a million flickering delusions, pinned to reels and circuits like gray-and-white butterflies on trays.

'Lovely,' says Motherwell, and opens fire.

(It's the seafront at Brighton. Frames wash over the shingle as the day falls, the birds fall, the skyline falls. 'Alpha Zero One. Ground Zero minus two miles.' 'Alpha Zero One. Ground Zero minus one mile.' The trees fall, the clouds fall, the word falls, the image falls. The bank drops into bottomless magnetic sound.

'Just telling you he kept –' 'Drop in sometime –' 'How much does it cost –' 'He showed no more emotion –' 'The Greek-key version of –'

Batman drops wordless, a phantom on the leafy bodies of Captain Marvel, the Green Hornet, Mandrake the Magician. The voices stir and die on long-forgotten cylinders. '– tough, urgent, gritty –' '– it's all a mistake –' '– sanctions will be imposed –' You remember 1967? You remember cold year? Could almost feel Cold Sun. Could almost feel the death of his images.)

That is how it has happened. It is four hours since Jack Beauregard was slain. His body is at St Mary Abbott's Hospital, at special request. There was some connection, which I never found out. They took him there in a large black Bentley with black tinted windows. They left him in the casualty ward and drove away without leaving their names.

He was not dead on arrival, but he said nothing. He died at 5:17pm without really recovering consciousness. He was said to be between 47 and 53 years old. It is hard to tell.

An impasse has been reached, for the moment. I sit at my desk and it's a summer evening. The sun is turning the roof tops orange. The clock has tricked me, as it always does. I wait for the phone to ring, and there will be more messages, and it will be time to go.

They are waiting, you see, for the next tactical movement to develop. For the time being, a problem has been solved. Beauregard is dead. Starfessed is saved, and Motherwell is once more in the wilderness. Honour, or something, is satisfied.

The others – they are not important. They wait like shadows for the next scene to begin. It will go on. The Programme of Sliced Man is not finished. This will not be the last we hear of John Remorse. We all have our jobs to do, and we must continue tomorrow.

Shack is here. He's staring out of the window for no reason at all. Macfries has gone home, and the cleaners are moving about his office with the sound of deer among leaves. A train honks, and rattles in the distance on its way to Clapham.

There is no need for résumé. I have written all I have to. The people are still here, they are still alive. They do not mean anything. Only Jack Beauregard means something, and we did not know him well. We are all tired, we must all rest now.

In the late sixties, Graham Masterton (wearing dark glasses) and William S Burroughs (wearing his distinctive hat) went to the Scientology Centre at Saint Hill in East Grinstead so that William could have a snoop around. They adopted the names of 'Graham Thomas' and 'William Lee'. This photograph was taken by another friend, film director and distributor Antony Balch. The woman in the picture was someone from the Scientology Centre.

ABOUT THE AUTHOR

Graham Masterton was born in Edinburgh on 16 January 1946.

After finishing his state education at the Whitgift school in Croydon, he worked for the *Crawley Observer* as a cub reporter and in 1967 applied to work for the *Daily Telegraph*, but was turned down. He then went to his uncle who worked on the *Evening Standard*, and was turned down again due to lack of experience. A day later his girlfriend suggested trying a new magazine called *Mayfair*. He applied and was hired.

As it turned out, he ended up doing virtually everything: writing the headlines, copy editing, typography – training which resulted in being able to write about anything at short notice.

After three years he moved over to the UK edition of *Penthouse*. The publishers had just started an American edition which led to Masterton visiting New York on a regular basis, getting to know the American publishers. With the support of those publishers he started writing sex instruction books.

In 1975 Masterton turned to horror. His first novel was *The Manitou*, and he followed that success with a stream of further titles.

In the eighties he diversified into writing historical sagas, thrillers, even movie tie-ins. Nowadays, he regularly contributes creative and instructive articles to magazines, and short stories to international anthologies and is still writing novels.

MORE TELOS TITLES

<u>HORROR/FANTASY</u>

<u>GRAHAM MASTERTON</u>
THE DJINN

<u>SIMON CLARK</u>
HUMPTY'S BONES
THE FALL

<u>SAM STONE</u>
ZOMBIES IN NEW YORK AND OTHER BLOODY
JOTTINGS
Horror Collection

KAT LIGHTFOOT MYSTERIES
Steampunk/Horror Series
ZOMBIES AT TIFFANY'S
KAT ON A HOT TIN AIRSHIP
WHAT'S DEAD PUSSYKAT

THE DARKNESS WITHIN
A thrilling sci-fi/horror novel

JINX CHRONICLES
Sci-Fi Post-Apocalyptic Trilogy
JINX TOWN - Book 1
JINX MAGIC - Book 2 (Coming in 2015)
JINX BOUND - Book 3 (Coming in 2016)

<u>DAVID J HOWE</u>
TALESPINNING
Horror collection of stories, extracts and screenplays

URBAN GOTHIC: LACUNA AND OTHER TRIPS edited by
DAVID J HOWE
Tales of horror from and inspired by the *Urban Gothic*
television series. Contributors: Graham Masterton,
Christopher Fowler, Simon Clark, Steve Lockley & Paul
Lewis, Paul Finch and Debbie Bennett.

RAVEN DANE
ABSINTHE & ARSENIC
16 tales of Victorian horror, Steampunk adventures and dark,
deadly, obsession

PRINCE OF RAVENS (Coming in 2015)
Exciting alternative history with a supernatural twist

KIT COX
DOCTOR TRIPPS SERIES
A Neo-Victorian world where steam is pitted against diesel,
but which side will win?
KAIJU COCKTAIL
MOON MONSTER (coming in 2015)

CAPTAINS STUPENDOUS by RHYS HUGHES
Steampunk humorous adventure about the Fantastical
Faraway Brothers

SPECTRE by STEPHEN LAWS
Something is stalking the Chapter, picking them off one by
one, something connected with their past, and with the girl
they used to know.
KING OF ALL THE DEAD by STEVE LOCKLEY & PAUL
LEWIS
The king of all the dead will have what is his.

THE HUMAN ABSTRACT by GEORGE MANN
A future tale of private detectives, AIs, Nanobots, love and
death.

BREATHE by CHRISTOPHER FOWLER
The Office meets *Night of the Living Dead*.

HOUDINI'S LAST ILLUSION by STEVE SAVILE
Can the master illusionist Harry Houdini outwit the dead
shades of his past?

ALICE'S JOURNEY BEYOND THE MOON by R J CARTER
A sequel to the classic Lewis Carroll tales.

APPROACHING OMEGA by ERIC BROWN
A colonisation mission to Earth runs into problems.

VALLEY OF LIGHTS by STEPHEN GALLAGHER
A cop comes up against a body-hopping murderer.

PRETTY YOUNG THINGS by DOMINIC MCDONAGH
A nest of lesbian rave bunny vampires is at large in
Manchester.

A MANHATTAN GHOST STORY by T M WRIGHT
Do you see ghosts? A classic tale of love and the
supernatural.

BLACK TIDE by DEL STONE JR
A college professor and his students find themselves trapped
by an encroaching horde of zombies following a waste
spillage.

FORCE MAJEURE by DANIEL O'MAHONY
An incredible fantasy novel.

SHROUDED BY DARKNESS: TALES OF TERROR edited by
ALISON L R DAVIES
An anthology of tales guaranteed to bring a chill to the spine.
This collection has been published to raise money for DebRA.
Featuring stories by: Debbie Bennett, Poppy Z Brite, Simon
Clark, Storm Constantine, Peter Crowther, Alison L R Davies,
Paul Finch, Christopher Fowler, Neil Gaiman, Gary
Greenwood, David J Howe, Dawn Knox, Tim Lebbon,
Charles de Lint, Steven Lockley & Paul Lewis, James
Lovegrove, Graham Masterton, Richard Christian Matheson,
Justina Robson, Mark Samuels, Darren Shan and Michael
Marshall Smith. With a frontispiece by Clive Barker and a
foreword by Stephen Jones. Deluxe hardback cover by Simon
Marsden.

CRIME

THE LONG, BIG KISS GOODBYE by SCOTT
MONTGOMERY
Hardboiled thrills as Jack Sharp gets involved with a dame
called Kitty.

ANDREW HOOK
A series of exciting crime novels putting a neo-noir twist on
the genre conventions of bums and dames
THE IMMORTALISTS
CHURCH OF WIRE (Coming 2015)

PRISCILLA MASTERS
Titles in Priscilla Masters' acclaimed Joanna Piercy series
1. WINDING UP THE SERPENT
2. CATCH THE FALLING SPARROW
3. A WREATH FOR MY SISTER
4. AND NONE SHALL SLEEP

MIKE RIPLEY

Titles in Mike Ripley's acclaimed 'Angel' series of comic
crime novels.
JUST ANOTHER ANGEL
ANGEL TOUCH
ANGEL HUNT
ANGEL ON THE INSIDE
ANGEL CONFIDENTIAL
ANGEL CITY
ANGELS IN ARMS
FAMILY OF ANGELS
BOOTLEGGED ANGEL
THAT ANGEL LOOK
ANGEL UNDERGROUND
LIGHTS, CAMERA, ANGEL

HANK JANSON

Classic pulp crime thrillers from the 1940s and 1950s.
TORMENT
WOMEN HATE TILL DEATH
SOME LOOK BETTER DEAD
SKIRTS BRING ME SORROW
WHEN DAMES GET TOUGH
ACCUSED
KILLER
FRAILS CAN BE SO TOUGH
BROADS DON'T SCARE EASY
KILL HER IF YOU CAN
LILIES FOR MY LOVELY
BLONDE ON THE SPOT
THIS WOMAN IS DEATH
THE LADY HAS A SCAR

TELOS PUBLISHING
Email: orders@telos.co.uk
Web: www.telos.co.uk

To order copies of any Telos books, please visit our website
where there are full details of all titles and facilities for
worldwide credit card online ordering, as well as
occasional special offers.